Praise for MALCOLM GL
from his

'I am a great wine lover and your book has enabled me to broaden my choice'

Mr M.G., Sheffield

'My husband was given a copy of *Superplonk 1997* . . . Life has not been the same since – supermarket shopping has been attractive – more power to your elbow (and ours!)'

Mrs A.H., Ratby, Leicestershire

'Malcolm Gluck, in his manifestation as *Superplonk*, has been a welcome, cheering and inebriating presence in my family since his first appearance'

Mr G.G., Newton Abbot

'Ever since I was given a present of your *Superplonk* book and thereby discovered your weekly column, I have not once been disappointed by your recommendations'

Mr J.W., Oxford

'It is a great help to be able to be pointed in the direction of a good 'glug' rather than stand dazed in front of rows and rows of appealing-looking labels . . . Wine is fun and so are your books'

Mr P.B., Shrewsbury

'Thank you again for the drinking pleasure your selections give us'

Mr A.W., Colchester

'Thank you for *Superplonk 1997*, essential reference for a totally ignorant wine buyer'

Mrs D.G.N., Uxbridge

'Incidentally, I treated myself pre-Christmas to a copy of the High Street guide, which I find equally enthralling! I fear that this will also become another annual "must have"'

Mrs B.F., Beckenham

'The moment you give a wine the magic score of 16 or above, it disappears entirely from the shelves'

Mr N.W., Cambridge

'May I sincerely thank you for a number of things: *Superplonk 1997*, *Streetplonk 1997* and *Gluck, Gluck, Gluck* . . . For the working man on a limited income as well as a person who appreciates value for money, your book has provided me with a genuine improvement of the quality of my life'

Mr R.J., Stoke Gifford

About the Author

Malcolm Gluck is the wine correspondent of the *Guardian*, mitigating the effects of tasting several thousand bottles of wine a year by cycling in all weathers all over London. He writes a weekly Saturday column, *Superplonk*. Last year he presented his own BBC-2 television series – *Gluck, Gluck, Gluck*. When he is not raising a glass, he helps raise a family.

Summerplonk 1997

Malcolm Gluck

CORONET BOOKS
Hodder and Stoughton

First published in Great Britain as
a Coronet paperback original in 1997

10 9 8 7 6 5 4 3 2 1

ISBN 0 340 69334 7

Typeset by Palimpsest Book Production Limited,
Polmont, Stirlingshire
Printed and bound in Great Britain by
Mackays of Chatham PLC, Chatham, Kent

Hodder and Stoughton
A division of Hodder Headline PLC
338 Euston Road
London NW1 3BH

To Sarah Lutyens – the paradox of great height
with greater depth

'I offer a bunch of pansies, not a wreath of immortelles'

D. H. Lawrence

CONTENTS

INTRODUCTION

Before you down a drop, please swallow these few words

My readers give me my living and in return I give my readers my liver. I've said this often enough in the past. So: you asked for a summer edition of *Superplonk* to augment the winter edition and here it is: *Summerplonk*.

The need for a second *Superplonk* book each year was evident to me a couple of years ago. However, I have fought shy of writing a second guide until now, because the extra work load seemed too daunting. Unlike other writers, whose workflow goes straight into a word-processor, mine first must make the journey down my gullet. But those who pay the plonker call the tune and I obey.

Every summer, the supermarkets put on sale an abundance of interesting wines which, like some of our more exotic insects, last only the brief months of the warmest months and then disappear. They never return. Thus these wines are listed in neither one year's *Superplonk* nor the succeeding one. To be sure, I write about these wines in my Saturday *Guardian* column but it has irked me that I have been unable, until this book, to give them their proper and most public airing – in a paperback book cheaply and widely available.

There are several reasons for the increase of seasonality with supermarket wine. It used to be the case that bargains bought specially – that is, tens of thousands of cases of wine negotiated at a rock bottom price with a winery or, more likely, a wine co-operative – appeared at Christmas when British wine drinkers are most boisterous. But the world of supermarket retailing has become increasingly competitive, ruthlessly so, and retailers want customers to favour them all year round. One obvious way to keep customers' curiosities alive is regularly to flaunt year-round bargains, special offers, and enticing new wines introduced at startlingly low prices.

This bustling arena has been given an additional (and most exciting) dynamic by the emergence in the past ten years of the New World of wine. Many of the countries able to bask under the exotic nomenclature of being a 'New World' wine producer harvest their grapes in our springtime and, especially with some red wines and wood-influenced whites, the latest vintages of their wines only emerge one year later – too late for the current edition of winter's *Superplonk* and too early for the edition to come. When I do come to finalise that new edition, many of these wines are in such short supply that I cannot list them in the book.

Summerplonk, then, is a very necessary publication for the dedicated superplonker.

It is also true that the older-established wine-producing countries, who process their grapes during the same autumn season as Britain's, also have bottled and ready for sale by the next spring some of their newest vintages. And here, too, this new crop has been swelled, in recent years, by the emergence of two new suppliers of wine to the UK. The first of these are the freshly energised regions of France, Spain, Italy and Portugal. The incursion of the so-called Flying Winemaker into hitherto backward wine regions along with the proliferation in these areas of New World wine techniques (such as cold fermentation, selected yeasts, new grape varieties, more adventurous blending, better vineyard and cellar management, more sophisticated soil maintenance techniques) has meant better wine – and more of it – becoming available to the professionals who buy wine for supermarkets. Indeed, increasingly these supermarkets take the lead in encouraging certain Old World wine regions to rediscover themselves; for these regions are almost invariably ones which for decades have been disdainfully sneered at by the fashionable wine areas (like Apulia in Italy thought of as barbarian by the Piedmontese, the Herault in southern France which is considered laughable in Bordeaux, and various previously inhospitable bits of the Spanish littoral which Riojans think fit only for growing firewood). These old regions, often with lurid and important histories, have commenced fresh careers purely as the result of British supermarkets' enthusiasms.

The second exciting new crop of wine regions are those in that part of Europe called Eastern (a term which will, I hope, fall into disuse once the next millennium gets under way and a new generation of politicians realises that divisions in the mind need as effectively erasing as those on paper or on land). Hungary, Romania, the Czech Republic, Bulgaria, Moldova, Moravia, and other parts of what was once pretentiously called the USSR as well as vineyards in what was once known as Yugoslavia, are all ancient producers of wine, and those which have been given a blood transfusion by the flushing out of poisonous political ideas are eager to sell wine to us. The regular annual springtime invasion of bottles from Europe, wine which barely six or eight months before was grapes on the vine, has been swelled by these regions, and here too many bottles only last the summer – or are only at their best and worth catching during that time.

It is true to say that many times wines do not make the winter *Superplonk*, because they have lost their edge since I first tasted them in spring. When I taste them again, nearer to publication time, arthritis has set in. Others which do make the book are not rated high enough to arouse drinkers' appetites. The publication of *Summerplonk* means that I can bring you these wines at the peak of their drinkability.

All this extra boozing has meant, naturally enough, a good deal more gargling, slurping, spitting and trips to the bottle bank. It has imposed on my dear wife an increased burden; even more than usual I have insisted on opening armfuls of wines with dinner and it has further meant more organisational and planning work for my shrewd strategist of an assistant Linda Peskin. It has also given the supermarket wine departments something to think about and they have buckled down, as ever, with patience and enthusiasm to meet my demands.

But, best of all, I hope this book will give you something to think about.

Health Warning!

I employed the emotive turn of phrase above in the book which accompanied my BBC-2 TV series last year. I feel no shame about borrowing from myself for this first edition of *Summerplonk.* Health Warning is an arresting phrase. And I hope by employing it I may save you from working yourself up into a state. Let me explain.

I get a few letters a week from readers (both column and book) telling me that a wine which I have said is on sale in a certain supermarket is not there and that either the wine has sold out or the branch claims to have no knowledge of it; I get letters telling me that a wine is a bit dearer than I said it was; and I get the odd note revealing that the vintage of the 16-point wine I have enthused about and which my correspondent desperately wants to buy is different from the one listed.

First of all, let me say that no wine guide in the short and inglorious history of the genre is more exhaustively researched, checked and double-checked than this one. I do not list a wine if I do not have assurances from its retailer that it will be widely on sale when the guide is published. Where a wine is on restricted distribution, or stocks are short and vulnerable to the assault of determined readers, I will always clearly say so. However, large retailers use computer systems which cannot anticipate uncommon demand and which often miss the odd branch off the anticipated stocking list. I cannot check every branch myself (though I do nose around them when I can) and so a wine in *Summerplonk* may well, maddeningly, be missing at the odd branch of its retailer and may not even have been heard of by the branch simply because of inhuman error. Conversely, the same technology often tells a retailer's head office that a wine is out of stock when it has merely been completely cleared out of the warehouse. It may still be on sale in certain branches. Then there is the fact that not every wine I write about is stocked by every single branch of its listed supermarket. Every store has what are called retail plans, and there may be half-a-dozen of these, and every wine is subject to a different stocking policy according to the dictates of these cold-hearted plans.

I accept a wine as being in healthy distribution if several hundred branches, all over the country, not just in selected parts of it, stock the wine. Do not assume, however, that this means every single branch has the wine.

I cannot, equally, guarantee that every wine in this book will still be in the same price band as printed (these bands follow this introduction). The vast majority will be. But there will always be the odd bottle from a country suddenly subject to a vicious swing in currency rates, or subject to an unprecedented rise in production costs which the supermarket cannot or is not prepared to swallow, and so a few pennies will get added to the price. If it is pounds, then you have cause for legitimate grievance. Please write to me. But don't lose a night's sleep if a wine is twenty pence more than I said it is. If you must, write to the appropriate supermarket. The department and the address to write to is provided with each supermarket's entry.

Now the puzzle of differing vintages. When I list and rate a wine, I do so only for the vintage stated. Any other vintage is a different wine requiring a new rating. Where vintages do have little difference in fruit quality, and more than a single vintage is on sale, then I say this clearly. If two vintages are on sale, and vary in quality and/or style, then they will be separately rated. However, be aware of one thing.

Superplonk is the biggest-selling wine guide to such an extent that all the other wine guides' sales put together do not reach even a fraction of it. I say this not to boast but, importantly, to acquaint you with a reality which may cause you some irritation. If *Summerplonk* sells well then there will be lots of eager drinkers aiming straight for the highest-rating wines as soon as possible after the book is published. Thus the supermarket wine buyer who assures me that she has masses of stock of Domaine Piddlewhatsit and the wine will withstand the most virulent of sieges may find her shelves emptying in a tenth of the time she banked on – not knowing, of course, how well I rate the wine until the book goes on sale. It is entirely possible, therefore, that the vintage of a highly rated wine may sell out so so quickly that new stocks of the follow-on vintage may be urgently brought on to shelf before I have tasted them. This can happen in some instances. I offer a bunch of pansies, not a wreath of immortelles. I can do nothing about this fact of wine-writing life, except to give up writing about wine.

Lastly, one thing more. And let me steal from myself yet again: '*Wine is a hostage to several fortunes (weather being even more uncertain and unpredictable than exchange rates) but the wine writer is hostage to just one: he cannot pour for his readers precisely the same wine as he poured for himself.*'

I wrote this last year and it holds true for every wine in this book and every wine I will write about in the years to come (for as long as my liver holds out). I am sent wines to taste regularly and I attend wine tastings all the time. If a wine is corked on these occasions, that is to say, not in good condition because it has been tainted by the tree bark which is its seal, then it is not a problem for a bottle in good condition to be quickly supplied for me to taste. This is not, alas, a luxury which can be extended to my readers.

So if you find a wine not to your taste because it seems pretty foul or off in some way, then do not assume that my rating system is up the creek; you may take it that the wine is faulty and must be returned as soon as possible to its retailer. Every retailer in this book is pledged to provide an instant refund for any faulty wine returned – no questions asked. I am not asking readers to share all my tastes in wine, or to agree completely with every rating for every wine. But where a wine I have rated well is obviously and patently foul, then it is a duff bottle and you should be compensated by getting a fresh bottle free or by being given a refund.

How I Rate a Wine

Each wine is rated on points out of 20. Wine names are as printed on the label. Each supermarket's wines are arranged by country of origin, red and white (including roses), with fortified and sparkling/champagne wines listed separately.

Value for money is my single unwavering focus. I drink with my readers' pockets in my mouth. I do not see the necessity of paying a lot for a bottle of everyday drinking wine and only rarely do I consider it worth paying a high price for, say, a wine for a special occasion or because you want to experience what a so-called 'grand' wine may be like. There is more codswallop talked and written about wine, especially the so-called 'grand' stuff, than any subject except sex. The stench of this gobbledegook regularly perfumes wine merchants' catalogues, spices the backs of bottles, and rancidises the writings of those infatuated by or in the pay of producers of a particular wine region. I do taste expensive wines regularly. I do not, regularly, find them worth the money. That said, there are some pricey bottles in these pages. They are here either because I wish to provide an accurate, but low, rating of its worth so that readers will be given pause for thought or because the wine is genuinely worth every penny. A wine of magnificent complexity, thrilling fruit, superb aroma, great depth and finesse is worth drinking. I would not expect it to be an inexpensive bottle. I will rate it highly. I wish all wines which commanded such high prices were so well deserving of an equally high rating. The thing is, of course, that many bottles of wine I taste do have finesse and depth but do not come attached to an absurdly high price tag. These are the bottles I prize most. As, I hope, you will.

20 Is outstanding and faultless in all departments: smell, taste and finish in the throat. Worth the price, even if you have to take out a second mortgage.

19 A superb wine. Almost perfect and well worth the expense (if it is an expensive bottle).

18 An excellent wine but lacking that ineffable sublimity of richness and complexity to achieve the very highest rating. But superb drinking and thundering good value.

17 An exciting, well-made wine at an affordable price which offers real glimpses of multi-layered richness.

16 Very good wine indeed. Good enough for any dinner party. Not expensive but terrifically drinkable, satisfying and multi-dimensional – properly balanced.

15 For the money, a good mouthful with real style. Good flavour and fruit without costing a packet.

14 The top end of the everyday drinking wine. Well-made and to be seriously recommended at the price.

13 Good wine, true to its grape(s). Not great, but certainly very drinkable.

12 Everyday drinking wine at a sensible price. Not exciting, but worthy.

11 Drinkable, but not a wine to dwell on. You don't wed a wine like this, though you might take it behind the bike shed with a bag of fish and chips.

10 Average wine (at a low price), yet still just about a passable mouthful. Also, wines which are terribly expensive and, though drinkable, cannot justify their high price.

9 Cheap plonk. Just about fit for parties in dustbin-sized dispensers.

8 On the rough side here.

7 Good for pickling onions or cleaning false teeth.

6 Hardly drinkable except as basic picnic plonk.

5 Wine with more defects than delights.

4 Not good at any price.

3 Barely drinkable.

2 Seriously – did this wine come from grapes?

1 The utter pits. The producer should be slung in prison.

The rating system above can be broken down into six broad sections.

Zero to 10:	Avoid – unless entertaining a stuffy wine writer.
10, 11:	Nothing poisonous but, though drinkable, rather dull.
12, 13:	Above average, interestingly made. Solid rather then sensational.
14,15,16:	This is the exceptional, hugely drinkable stuff, from the very good to the brilliant.
17, 18:	Really wonderful wine worth anyone's money: complex, rich, exciting.
19,20:	A toweringly brilliant world-class wine of self-evident style and individuality.

Prices

It is impossible to guarantee the price of any wine in this guide. This is why instead of printing the shop price, each wine is given a price band. This attempts to eliminate the problem of printing the wrong price for a wine. This can occur for all the usual boring but understandable reasons: inflation, economic conditions overseas, the narrow margins on some supermarket wines making it difficult to maintain consistent prices and, of course, the existence of those freebooters at the Exchequer who are liable to inflate taxes which the supermarkets cannot help but pass on. But even price banding is not foolproof. A wine listed in the book at, say, a B band price might be on sale at a C band price. How? Because a wine close to but under, say, £3.50 in spring when I tasted it might sneak across the border in summer. It happens, rarely enough not to concern me overmuch, but wine is an agricultural import, a sophisticated liquid food, and that makes it volatile where price is concerned. Frankly, I admire the way retailers have kept prices so stable for so many years. We drink cheaper (and healthier) wine now than we did thirty years ago.The price banding code assigned to each wine works as follows:

Price Band

A Under £2.50	B £2.50 to £3.50	C £3.50 to £5
D £5 to £7	E £7 to £10	F £10 to £13
G £13 to £20	H Over £20	

All wines costing under £5 (i.e. A–C) have their price band set against a black background.

ACKNOWLEDGEMENTS

Ivory towers are not congenial habitats for the active wine writer. Poets may yearn for them, but I could not put this little volume together were it not for an understanding family, a wonderful assistant, an indulgent editor (and marvellously accommodating printer), a superb copy editor, and lots of jolly people backing up my efforts at Hodder & Stoughton. I owe thanks, therefore, to Linda Peskin, Helen Dore, George Lucas and Kate Lyall Grant, Martin Neild, Kerr MacRae, Jamie Hodder-Williams, Karen Geary, Katie Gunning and typesetter Craig Morrison.

ASDA

ARGENTINIAN WINE RED

Argentinian Red 1996, Asda 

Very willing to please. Terrific rich, ripe fruit.

La Rural Mendoza Malbec 1996 

Vivacity, style, richness, flavour and oodles of pizzazz. This is soft, big and exceedingly drinkable.

ARGENTINIAN WINE WHITE

Argentinian White 1996, Asda 

Solid thwack of flavour, soft and very full. Delicious richness and texture.

La Rural Mendoza Pinot Blanc/Chardonnay 1996  

AUSTRALIAN WINE RED

Chateau Reynella Basket Press Shiraz 1994  

The richness of this wine is not superficial but committed and deep. It is an outstanding Aussie.

Chateau Reynella Basket-Pressed Cabernet/Merlot 1994 16 E

Ripe cabernet and soft leathery merlot deliciously combine both aromatically and fruit-wise in layers of rich flavours. A very convincing wine. Sheer satiny class.

Hardys Bankside Shiraz 1995 14 D

Wins on its approach, rather than its quiet departure.

Hardys Nottage Hill Cabernet Sauvignon/ Shiraz 1994 15 C

Penfolds Bin 28 Kalimna Shiraz 1994 14 E

Expensive but very impressively fruity and fine. Both dry and flavourful.

Penfolds Rawson's Retreat Bin 35 Cabernet/Shiraz 1995 13.5 C

Peter Lehmann Vine Vale Grenache 1996 14 C

Soft, aromatic, ripe, tasty. Perhaps too accommodating to instant likeability to handle robust food.

Rosemount Estate Shiraz 1994 14 D

Rosemount Shiraz/Cabernet 1995 15 C

South Australian Cabernet Sauvignon 1994 13.5 C

South Eastern Australia Shiraz/Cabernet 1996, Asda 13 B

Curiously light-minded and unadventurous.

AUSTRALIAN WINE — WHITE

Chateau Reynella Chardonnay 1995 16.5 E

Superb texture, fruit, flavour, balance and lush yet sophisticated style. It is one of the best vintages of one of Australia's tastiest chardonnays.

Cranswick Oak Aged Marsanne 1995 16 C

Waxy, rich, aromatic, with loads of smoky fruit, dollops of jammy flavour underneath, and a lime finish. Terrific summer food wine.

Geoff Merrill Sauvignon/Semillon 1996 14 C

Layers of lemony fruit tickle the palate and engage brilliantly with fish dishes.

Hardys Nottage Hill Chardonnay 1995 15.5 C

Hardys Stamp of Australia Grenache/ Shiraz Rose 1996 11.5 C

Hardys Stamp of Australia Riesling/ Traminer 1996 14.5 C

Deliciously complex, quirkily, subtly exotic and great for Thai and Chinese fish and chicken dishes.

Jackdaw Ridge Australian White 11 B

Kingston Chenin Verdelho 1996 15 C

Good with Thai food and barbecued prawns. Has a waxy apricot edge to its citric fruit (subtle). Good glugging.

Kingston Semillon/Verdelho 1996 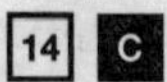

Great shellfish wine. Has a lovely cleanness of crisp fruit.

Penfolds Barossa Valley Semillon/ Chardonnay 1995 

Classy stuff: achingly toothsome fruit, shrouded in smoky melon and pear.

Penfolds Bin 202 Rhine Riesling 1996 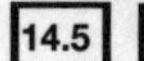 

Interesting softish fruit with a crisp pineapple tang. Will develop well in bottle over the next year.

Penfolds Rawsons Retreat Bin 21 Semillon/Chardonnay/Colombard 1996 

Richly textured, warmly fruity (some complexity on the finish where the acidity is most pertinent), this is an excellent vintage for this wine.

Peter Lehmann The Barossa Semillon 1996 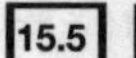 

Has a lush richness, beautiful cool texture and a solid finish. A truly flavourful wine. Great with all sorts of barbecued food.

Rosemount Estate Chardonnay 1995  

Beautiful controlled fruit with vivacity and restraint. This paradox is Rosemount's hallmark.

Rosemount Estate Semillon/Chardonnay 1996 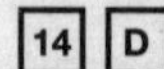

Elegance personified.

South Australian Chardonnay 1995, Asda 16 C

Fabulous bottle of rich, full, deep, beautifully arranged chardonnay with oodles of flavour and richness. Solid quaffing wine as well as sufficiently brawny to lift food. Excellent price.

South East Australian Semillon Chardonnay 1996, Asda 

A lighter style of Aussie – but a refreshing one.

BULGARIAN WINE — RED

Bulgarian Vintage Premium Merlot 1994 13 B

Liubimetz Merlot Premiere 1994 16 B

Stunning value. Lovely ripe fruit, soft as crumpled satin, with good tannins and acidity. Has depth, style and flavour – and an astounding price.

CHILEAN WINE — RED

Alto Plano Chilean Red 15 B

Chilean Cabernet/Merlot 1995, Asda 16.5 C

The new vintage has a gorgeous lingering flavour of coffee, walnut and plum. The texture and depth of fruit is extraordinary for the money.

Cono Sur Cabernet Sauvignon 1994 15 C

Rowanbrook Cabernet Sauvignon Reserve 1994 14 C

Rowanbrook Cabernet Sauvignon/Malbec 1996 14 B

Dry, flavourful, fruitily well-organised.

Rowanbrook Zinfandel 1996 13.5 C

Soft, zippy, amusing.

Terra Noble Merlot 1995 16 C

Superb richness of corduroy-textured, thickly woven fruit. Quite stunning depth of flavour.

Valdivieso Malbec 1996 17.5 C

Wonderful wine! Quite wonderful! The texture is the softest velvet, the fruit is exquisite plum and blackberry, the balance is poised.

CHILEAN WINE WHITE

Alto Plano Chilean White 12 B

Chilean Sauvignon Blanc 1996, Asda 14 B

Cono Sur Chilean Chardonnay 1995 14 C

Rowanbrook Chardonnay Reserve 1995 16 C

Deliciousness personified. Come home from work, stretch out your legs, kick off your shoes and relax.

Rowanbrook Sauvignon Blanc Reserve 1996 14.5 C

Lots of flavour relieved, deftly, by a rich, acidic vein. Classy feel.

Valdivieso Chardonnay 1996 16.5 C

Wonderful richness of complexity and length of flavour. Balanced, elegant, vivid (yet soft and ripe), hugely stylish and totally captivating.

Vina Porta Chardonnay Reserve 1995 14 D

Softness yet pointed and fine on the finish. Not as complex as many other Chilean chardonnays at this price, though.

FRENCH WINE RED

Beaujolais, Asda 12 C

Beaujolais Villages Domaine des Ronzes 1995 13.5 C

Buzet Cuvee 44 1996 13 C

Almost rough and not quite ready.

Cabernet Sauvignon VdP d'Oc, Asda 15 B

Cahors, Asda 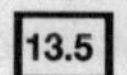

Chateau de Parenchere Bordeaux Superieur 1995 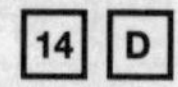

An approachable claret but with serious hints of class and depth. Good with food.

Chateau Fonfroide Bordeaux 1996 

Dry, brisk, charcoal-edged fruit of classic bordeaux go-to-hell stylishness. Great with lamb chops (well-burned ones).

Chateau l'Eglise Vieille, Haut Medoc 1995 

Very classy stuff: dry, chocolatey, full of itself, yet very rich and satisfying. An elegant, very gripping claret at a down-to-earth price.

Chateau la Domeque, Corbieres 1993 

Chateau Peybonnehomme Les Tours Cotes de Blaye 1994 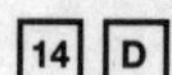

Ready, rich, dry, very, very attractive.

Chateauneuf-du-Pape 1996 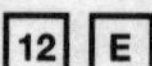

Not convinced by this. It's a mucked-about-with Chateauneuf. Like seeing racing stripes on a Fiat 500.

Claret, Asda  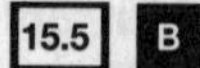

Cotes du Rhone Villages Domaine de Belugue 1994 

Brilliant, New World sweetness and lushness with big Old World tannins. Lovely wine. Emphatic concentration of flavour here.

Domaine de Grangeneuve, Coteaux du Tricastin 1995 15 C

Dry, earthy, blackcurranty, well-balanced and priced – this is a solid, soft, vital Rhone.

Domaine de la Baume Merlot VdP 1993 17 D

Quite brilliant balance of fruit and acidity and tannin. A bustling, handsome brute with couth manners and massive richness. For the money, one of France's finest merlots.

Domaine de la Baume Merlot VdP d'Oc 1994 17 D

One of the tastiest merlots on sale. World-class. Almost perfect precision.

Fitou, Asda 14 B

James Herrick 'Cuvee Simone' VdP 1994 17.5 C

A wine to love for its rocky, sun-drenched fruit and compacted herbiness. Very tannic and rich, it'll improve for a few years.

La Domeq Syrah Vieilles Vignes 'Tete de Cuvee' 1995 16 D

Delicious through-put of flavour here: dry yet ripe, rich, multi-layered fruit of substance, flavour and charm.

Mas Segala Cotes du Roussillon Villages 1996 13.5 C

Not as richly fruity or textured as previous vintages. It may be the wine is young, but I wonder if it will improve dramatically.

Merlot, Vin de Pays d'Oc, Asda 15 B

Montagne Noire Rouge VdP de l'Aude 1996 14 B

Rich, earthy, dry, convincing. Well-priced and packed with flavour.

Montagne Noire Syrah/Merlot 1995 14.5 B

Oak Aged Cotes du Rhone 1996, Asda 13 C

Light with earthy overtones. Not bad, but it seems to be straining for effect.

Red Burgundy 1995, Asda 11 C

St Chinian, Asda 14 B

Tramontane Grenache VdP d'Oc 1996 13.5 B

Soft and earthless. Curious aroma of stale eggs.

Tramontane Syrah VdP d'Oc 1996 13 B

Dry yet trying to be fruitier. Not entirely convincing.

FRENCH WINE WHITE

Bin 050 Sauvignon Blanc/Carignan 1996 14 B

An organic wine with an earthy edge to its tingling, fruity freshness. Good with food and fellowship.

Chablis 1995, Asda 13 E

Expensive, but hints of class give it some merit.

Chablis Premier Cru Les Fourchaumes 1995 14 F

Expensive, yes, very expensive, but it is on form: clean, delicately fruity with a clean finish, and nicely balanced.

Chardonnay, Vin de Pays d'Oc, Asda 14.5 C

Chateau la Blanquerie Entre Deux Mers 1995 14 C

Cotes de Bergerac 'Confit de la Colline' 1995 (half bottle) 15 D

Cotes du Rhone Blanc Chateau du Trignon 1995 15.5 D

Cuckoo Hill Viognier VdP d'Oc 1996 13.5 C

Crisp with an apricot edge which though an echo of a full-blooded viognier is nevertheless charming. I just wish it was a quid cheaper.

Domaine de Trignon Cotes du Rhone 1996 14.5 D

I love the quaint thatched roof on this solid modern edifice. It's a crisp modern piece of architecture, in other words, with a characterful finish.

Domaine des Deux Roches St Veran 1996 15 D

Expensive but very classy, very delicious. A gentle opulence to the fruit surprises and delights.

James Herrick Chardonnay VdP d'Oc 1996 14.5 C

New World restrained by Old World coyness. A chardonnay of subtlety and crisp fruit which is always nicely understated.

La Domeq 'Tete de Cuvee' Blanc 1996 15.5 C

Old French style in a hippy treatment of new-fangled wine-making. It's faintly luscious, quite elegant and very crisp to finish.

Macon-Vinzelles Les Cailloux 1996 14.5 D

Creamy, mildly lemonic with a nutty smoke undertone, this is a very tasty Macon blanc of very pretty fruit.

Montagne Noire Chardonnay, VdP d'Oc 1996 15 C

Excellent value for such ripe fruit in excellent form. It's well textured yet never too full or rich. It's a terrific summer tipple.

Montagne Noire Sauvignon Blanc 1996 13.5 B

Very clean – perhaps a bit touchy about releasing its fruit.

Muscadet de Sevre et Maine Sur Lie, Domaine Gautron 1995 11 C

Rather numbed – as if in mourning for long-dead fruit.

Pouilly Fume, Domaine Coulbois 1995 13 E

I like it but not so much that I'd enthusiastically pay £7.75 for it.

Premieres Cotes de Bordeaux Blanc, Asda 14 C

A sweet wine at an accommodating price which has enough

depth and richness to serve as an after-dinner glass with a goat's cheese and a bunch of grapes.

Sancerre Domaine de Sarry 1996 13.5 D

Far from indecent if not especially exciting value.

Sauvignon de Bordeaux, Asda 14.5 B

Spring Vale Blanc VdP 1995 13.5 B

Vin de Pays des Cotes de Gascogne, Asda 15 B

Citric pineapple gives it a slightly exotic edge. A super warm-weather aperitif.

Vouvray Denis Marchais Hand Picked 1996 15.5 C

Yes, it's off-dry, even a touch honeyed. But it's a wonderful summer aperitif: individual, rich, enticing, ripe, invigorating, floral.

GERMAN WINE WHITE

Hochheimer Holle Riesling Kabinett Aschrott 1995 12 D

Give it two to three years to show itself more vividly.

Northern Star Dry White 1996 13 B

Faintly floral, attempts at crispness, almost succeeds.

Northern Star Medium Dry White 1996 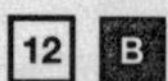

Sweet, but good for Lieb lovers looking for a way out.

Ruppertsberger Nussbein Riesling Auslese 1993 (50cl) 13.5 C

St Ursula Deidesheimer Hofstuck Kabinett 1994 13.5 B

Villa Eden Vineyards Riesling Kabinett QMP 1996 11 C

Odd and a little empty.

Wild Boar Vineyards Riesling 1996 

If this is the way new-style, dry, crisp but faintly floral German rieslings can go, then all power to their elbow and full glasses to ours!

GREEK WINE RED

Marble Mountain Cabernet/St George 1996 15.5 B

A wonderful surprise to anyone who thought the Greeks had lost the art of growing rich, characterful wine grapes about the time Aristotle died.

Temple Ruins Greek Red 1996 

Brilliant summer drinking, chilled with food, or merely with the Sunday papers.

GREEK WINE WHITE

Marble Mountain Roditis/Chardonnay 1996 13.5 B

Somewhat muddy edge to the fruit fails to mark it higher.

Temple Ruins Greek White 1996 14 B

Has a smoky melon edge to the creamy fruit. First-rate tippling here.

HUNGARIAN WINE WHITE

Deer Ridge Oak Aged Chardonnay 1996 15.5 C

Utterly delicious richness, texture and flavour. Creamy yet ripe, smoky yet fresh, this is a great bottle for summer foods.

Deer Ridge Sauvignon Blanc/Traminer 1996 13.5 B

A very pleasant tipple – if not exciting.

Mecsekalji Chardonnay Reserve 1996 14 B

Attractive simplicity and directness. A soft engaging wine.

Sopron Sauvignon Blanc Reserve 1996 14 B

Keen and grassy, great with barbecued mackerel.

ITALIAN WINE RED

Barolo, Veglio Angelo 1993 13.5 E

Dry and tasty – but expensive.

Chianti Colli Senesi Salvanza 1995 13 C

Coltiva Il Rosso 1996 12 B

Very light and coltish.

Due Rossi Merlot/Refosco 1996 13 C

La Vis Pinot Nero 1995 13 C

Light! Touch too light!

Lambrusco Rosso, Asda 12 A

Montepulciano d'Abruzzo, Cantina Tollo 1996 13.5 B

Pleasant, light, drinkable.

Rozzano Villa Pigna 1996 15.5 C

Rich, finely sculpted fruit of finesse and style. Lovely texture. A terrific wine.

Sicilian Rosso, Asda 16.5 B

New blend of an old favourite, which hit a low sweet note last year, but it's back to form with oodles of soft, rich fruit, a tannic touch on the finish and a very good grip. Terrific value. Fun slurping.

Valpolicella Classico 'Sanroseda' 1996 13 C

Light and somewhat expensive.

Valpolicella NV, Asda 11 B

ITALIAN WINE WHITE

Cantina Rosata 12 B

Coltiva Il Bianco 1996 14.5 B

Honey and ripe melon finish it off. An excellent glug for June lunches.

Due Bianchi Sauvignon/Pinot Bianco 1996 13.5 C

Not bad, but the price seems steep.

La Vis Trentino Chardonnay 1996 12.5 C

La Vis Valdadige Pinot Grigio 1996 14 C

Delicious, clean and crisp. Like a sushi chef's knife edge (sans fish).

Lambrusco Bianco, Asda 12.5 A

Lambrusco Rosato, Asda 12 A

Lambrusco Secco, Asda 11 A

Recioto di Soave Castelcerino 1993 (half bottle) 14 C

Sicilian Bianco, Asda 13.5 B

Soave, Asda 12.5 B

Soave Classico 'Sanroseda' 1996 13.5 C

Not bad, but £3.99 is asking for trouble.

MOROCCAN WINE RED

Domaine Mellil Moroccan Red Wine 15 B

PORTUGUESE WINE RED

Bright Brothers 'Old Vines' Estramadura 1995 13.5 C

Soft and ripe.

Bright Brothers Trincadeira 1996 13 C

Very light and puppyish sort of wine.

PORTUGUESE WINE WHITE

Fiuza Barrel Fermented Chardonnay 1995 16 C

Woody undertone gives this wine purpose and style. Good fruit well coated in flavoursomeness which finishes very elegantly.

Fiuza Sauvignon Blanc 1996 16 C

Gorgeous, rich, inviting aroma. Big opulent fruit of textured tautness yet suppleness. Soft finish. Lovely glug.

Vinho Verde, Asda 11 B

ROMANIAN WINE — WHITE

River Route Sauvignon/Muscat 1994 12.5 B

SOUTH AFRICAN WINE — RED

Athlone Pinotage 1996 13.5 C

Juicy, rather than gripping in the usual whizzbang pinotage fashion.

Bouwland Bush Vine Pinotage 1995 16.5 C

Drink it quickly before the pinotage fruit fades (it is a grape variety, like *Baywatch* babes and peeled avocados, which ages poorly). Offers plums and blackberries in its complex fruit salad of flavours, very fruity but never sweet, and a concentrated finish of black cherry.

Cape Red, Asda 15 B

Fairview Estate Cabernet Sauvignon Reserve 1995 13 D

Oddly jammy and juicy cabernet.

Fairview Estate Dry Red 1996 

Very juicy and ripe. Great for pasta parties.

Fairview Estate Shiraz 1995 16.5 C

Simply superb, the way it gets more and more complex from aroma, through the tastebuds, down the throat, and still lingers on the teeth for several minutes. Chocolate, spices, rich damsons, figs and a hint of coffee, this is some shiraz. Not remotely like any Aussie you've ever tasted.

Jennsberg Pinot Noir 1996 14 C

This is not at all a bad stab at pinot. Makes you wonder what they do to make it taste like it does in Burgundy.

Kanonkop Bouwland Red 1994 14 C

Kumala Shiraz/Cabernet Sauvignon 1996 14.5 B

Landskroon Cabernet Franc 1996 13.5 B

Dry and almost a candidate for higher honours – but it just seems too anxious to please.

Landskroon Pinotage 1995 13 C

Savanha Pinotage/Cabernet 1996 13.5 C

Savanha Vineyards Western Cape Shiraz 1996 13 C

Stellenzicht Block Zinfandel 1995 16.5 C

Lovely depraved stuff!!! Rich and rounded, vigorous and purposeful, this is a terrifically fulfilling wine. It oozes fruit, style and depth. Has a brazen, bawdy edge.

SOUTH AFRICAN WINE WHITE

Benguela Current Western Cape Chardonnay 1996 13 C

Cape White, Asda 13.5 B

Fairview Estate Dry Rose 1996 16 C

Possibly the best rose around four quid. Loads of flavour, crisply conceived yet full, and a brilliant finish.

Fairview Estate Dry White 1996 14 C

Crisp and fresh, almost springy-dry like after an early morning shower but with an exotic lemony hint. Good with food.

Fairview Estate Gewurztraminer 1996 14 C

A lightly spicy gewurz – strong on clean, crisp fruit – and it's great with fish.

Kumala Chenin/Chardonnay 1996 13.5 B

Muscat de Frontignan Danie de Wet 1996 16.5 C

Only Asda has this wine and all credit to them! A magnificently different aperitif: sweet, honeyed, floral, beautifully balanced and finely cut. A great summer drink. Dare to be sweet this season!!

Savanha Benguela Current Chardonnay 1996 16 C

Nutty, aromatic, rich, ripe, balanced, swimming in fruit but controlled and finely cut and very firm to finish. Very elegant tippling here.

Savanha Sauvignon Blanc 1996 

Flavour, texture, style – a touch expensive close to a fiver, perhaps, since these three virtues are subtly conceived. But the quality is there.

Van Loveren Sauvignon Blanc 1996 

SPANISH WINE RED

Baron de Ley Rioja Reserva 1991 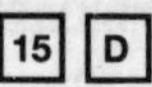

Expensive but a ripely fruity wine with great classiness. Oodles of flavour.

Bodegas Campillo, Rioja Crianza 1993 

Creamy, banana-y, vanilla-edged red of great interest to barbecue lighters – with meats it'll be terrific.

Don Darias 

El Meson Rioja CVC 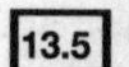

Remonte Navarra Tinto 1995 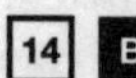

Terra Alta Cabernet Sauvignon/Garnacha 1995 15 B

Terra Alta 'Old Bush Vines' Garnacha 1996 

Soft, ripe, very ready. Has a good earthy touch to it and is a solid glugger and food contender.

Valencia Red, Asda 14 B

Vina Albali, Valdepenas Reserva 1989 15 B

SPANISH WINE WHITE

La Mancha, Asda 12 A

Moscatel de Valencia, Asda 14 B

Remonte Navarra Blanco 1995 11 B

Valdoro Tierra de Barros Spanish Country White 1996 15 B

Brilliant summer tippling. Clean fruit with a gentle peachy edge. Bargain barbecue bottle.

Valencia Dry, Asda 12 B

Valencia Medium Dry, Asda 11 B

USA WINE RED

California Red, Asda 14 B

Grant Canyon Select Red (California) 14 C

Quivira Cabernet Cuvee 1992 16 D

Packed with wild herbs and earthy, faintly spicy, cassis-edged fruit. Brilliant stuff.

Talus Californian Merlot 1995 13 D

So mild-mannered it makes you want to strangle the bottle by the neck.

USA WINE — WHITE

Californian White, Asda 13 B

Grant Canyon Californian White 10.5 C

Talus California Chardonnay 1996 15.5 C

Masses of flavour – like a high-class sweetshop (yet a dry one).

FORTIFIED WINE

Amarone della Valpolicella Sanroseda 1993 (50cl) 15 D

A real treat for the solo hedonist with a book in a deckchair. A ripe, off-dryish, figgy (yet dry to finish) wine of quaintness and rich insistence of flavour.

Fine Ruby Port, Asda 13.5 

LBV Port, Asda 13 C

Stanton & Killeen, Liqueur Muscat, Rutherglen (half bottle) 15 D

A rich, sweet, hugely all-embracingly ripe wine of great companionship qualities with summer pudding.

Tawny Port, Asda 14 D

Vintage Character Port, Asda 14 D

SPARKLING WINE/CHAMPAGNE

Asti Spumante, Asda 12 C

Barramundi Australian Brut 15.5 D

Blue Ridge Australian Brut 13 C

Cava Brut, Asda 14.5 C

Cava Rosado, Asda 15 C

Champagne Brut, Asda 13.5 F

The lighter style, modern and petticoaty, less serious.

Champagne Rose, Asda 12.5 F

Cordoniu Chardonnay Brut (Spain) 16 D

Delicious, classy, lively aperitif or to be drunk with smoked fish.

Cordoniu Premier Cuvee Brut (Spain) 14 D

Cranswick Pinot/Chardonnay Brut (Australia) 15 D

Wonderful summery bubbly of class and lemonic incisiveness. Delicious.

Nicholas Feuillate Blanc de Blancs NV 15 G

One of the most delicately citric and delicious champagnes around. Expensive elegance.

Scharffenberger Brut (USA) 13.5 E

Expensive, when Cava's as good at half the price.

Seaview Rose Brut 15 D

Wonderful summery rose. Quite delicious.

Veuve Clicquot Yellow Label Brut NV 12 H

I wouldn't pay twenty-two quid for it – in spite of its dry drinkability.

Vintage Champagne 1990, Asda 12 G

You get a free gift tin with this wine. It's hollow.

Asda Stores Limited
Asda House
Great Wilson Street
Leeds LS11 5AD
Tel 0113 2435435
Fax 0113 2418146

Summerplonk 1997

BOOTHS

ARGENTINIAN WINE RED

Libertad Sangiovese Malbec 1996 13 C

Nice plump texture and soft fruit.

Mission Peak Red 13 B

Dry, rather austere.

Valle de Vistalba, Barbera 1995 14.5 C

Lovely mixed blessing of sunshine, herbs, textured fruit and depth.

ARGENTINIAN WINE WHITE

Libertad Chenin Blanc 1996 14 C

Unusually delicious, cloying edge of the fruit makes this a mannered wine but one of charm.

AUSTRALIAN WINE RED

Brown Brothers Tarrango 1996 13.5 D

I just wish it were under four quid, this rubbery, aromatic, soft, well-flavoured wine. It is very versatile, meat or fish, and chills uncomplainingly.

Penfolds Bin 407 Cabernet Sauvignon 1993

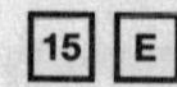

Ripe fruit, sound tannins, richness and flavour. A sedate yet invigorating cabernet of style and elegance.

Penfolds Rawsons Retreat Bin 35 1995

Respectable rather than raunchy.

Plantagenet Mount Barker Shiraz 1994

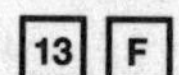

Lovely texture and fruit quality as it enters the mouth but it doesn't give the throat much to enjoy.

Riddoch Cabernet Shiraz, Coonawarra 1994

Falls away at the end a bit – shouldn't at this price.

Rosemount Estate Shiraz/Cabernet 1996

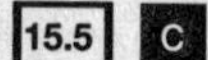

So soft and slip-downable it may be a crime.

AUSTRALIAN WINE WHITE

Barramundi Semillon/Colombard/ Chardonnay NV

The ultimate jazzy summery label fronts the ultimate jazzy summer wine. Drink it out of a bucket. A mere glass is too restricting.

Booth's Estate Semillon

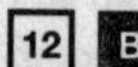

David Wynn Dry White 1995 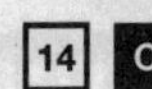

A light summer quaff with enough of a lilt on the finish to encourage tumultuous encores.

David Wynn Riesling, Eden Valley 1995 

Not a typical riesling, and rather highly priced, but decent enough.

Deakin Estate Chardonnay, Victoria 1996 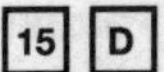

Oooh, it's luscious and scrumptiously put together. If you must be extravagant with your chardonnay this specimen would be worth maybe 18 points under a fiver.

Kingston Chenin Verdelho 1995 

Quirky citric fruit with a fat-edged finish. Touch apricoty? Perhaps. Makes a good appetite-whetter.

Penfolds Rawsons Retreat Bin 202 Riesling 1996  

Words fail me. (I should never have had the second bottle.)

Penfolds Rawsons Retreat Bin 21 Semillon/Chardonnay/Colombard 1996 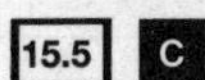 

Loaded with flavour and rich layers of fruit, it is nevertheless difficult to justify paying more for a summer wine.

Riddoch Chardonnay, Coonawarra 1994 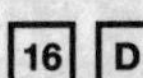

One of the most elegantly shaped of Aussie chardonnays: smoky, rich, beautifully balanced, finely poised twixt fruit and acid. It's gorgeous and well worth seven quid.

CHILEAN WINE RED

Carmen Reserve Grande Vidure Cabernet, Maipo 1995 16 D

One of Chile's most velvety, most flavour-packed yet elegant red wines. It is immensely classy and drinkable.

Palmeras Oak Aged Cabernet Sauvignon, Santa Emiliana 1995 16 C

Rich, ready, textured, very classy, this is a terrific cab for the money. It is a tasty tipple with or without food.

Tierra del Rey Chilean Red 15 B

Good evolved tannins, excellent depth of fruit with alert acidity, and a decent finish of no-hurry-to-quit demeanour. It is immensely drinkable, likeable, charming and good with food.

Vina Linderos Cabernet Sauvignon 15.5 D

Curious specimen of richness and softness. Has lush texture yet serious, chocolate-edged, cassis fruit. Really quite unusually delicious.

CHILEAN WINE WHITE

Andes Peak Chardonnay 1996 15 C

Fills the mouth with an opulence of flavour and ripeness which is scandalously stimulating. Be careful if you offer it to the neighbours. They may stay the night.

ENGLISH WINE — WHITE

Epoch V Chapel Down 1995

One of the United Kingdom's most drinkable under-a-fiver bottles. Falls away a bit on the finish, though.

Partnership Dry White, English Winegrowers NV

Can't see it myself. The dryness, I mean. But it's very pleasant to sip with foreign riff-raff as company to demonstrate the truth of the greenhouse effect on southern England.

FRENCH WINE — RED

Abbaye St Hilaire, Coteaux Varois 1994

Bourgogne Pinot Noir, Cave de Lugny 1994 11 D

Cahors, Cotes d'Olt 1994

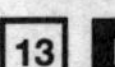

Needs a couple of hours of opening to get it into shape.

Chateau de Canterrane 1980 13.5 D

Chateau du Junca, Haut Medoc 1990 14.5 E

Chateau la Ferme d'Angludet, Margaux 1993 12 E

Chateau Tourt Choilet, Graves 1990 10 E

Cote Rotie La Garde 1987 10 G

Cotes de St Mont, Roc des Termes 1994 13 C

Dry and gently earthy.

Cotes du Brulhois, Cave de Donzac 1990 14 C

Good dry, herby fruit with decently developed tannins. Excellent with barbecued meats.

Cotes du Ventoux La Falaise 1995 13 B

Only a light cliff to ascend here.

Domaine de Belvezet VdP des Coteaux de l'Ardeche 1995 13 C

Good upfront fruit but a rather sissy finish.

Echezeaux, Domaine de la Romanee Conti 1990 10 H

Faugeres Gilbert Alquier 1994 14 D

You may say that seven quid for a country bumpkin is a bit rich. And you'd be right. This wine is richer and better than any claret.

Gamay Jardin de la France 11 B

Julienas Paul Boutinot 1995 12 D

Mature Margaux Chateau Brane-Cantenac 1977 12 F

Lovely tobacco aroma, but the fruit isn't so surprising or brilliant.

Nicole Rouge 8 B

Oak-Aged Claret, Booths 12 C

Reserve de Reverend Corbieres Rouge 1994 14 B

Volnay Joseph Drouhin 1989 10 G

Vosne Romanee Cacheux 1991 10 G

FRENCH WINE WHITE

Bergerac Blanc, Booths 14 B

Caves de Berticot Sauvignon Blanc 1994 13.5 C

Caves de Berticot Cotes de Duras Sauvignon 1995 14.5 C

Simply superb clean fresh fruit with sufficient flavour to accompany all fish dishes.

Chapelle de Cray Sauvignon Touraine 1994 13 C

Chateau Lamothe Vincent Bordeaux 1996 

A lovely white bordeaux in the classic Graves style: fresh and mineral-edged. Great with shellfish.

Cuvee Classique VdP des Cotes de Gascogne 1996 15.5 B

I love the impishness of white Gascons when they present such easy-drinking, delicious, pineapple-edged fruit. A superb summer aperitif.

Gaillac Blanc Hardys 1995 13.5 C

Gewurztraminer Turckheim 1995 15 D

Okay, spoil your back-garden buddies with this rose-petal fruity wine. It's delicious, exotic, Thai food-friendly.

James Herrick Chardonnay 1995 15 C

Muscadet sur Lie Domaine du Roc 1995 11.5 C

No, no, I'm being mean. Make it 12 points.

Nicole Blanc 9 B

Pinot Blanc Caves de Turckheim 1995 15.5 C

Wonderful price for a terrific pinot of richness and style which will develop well for a couple of years.

Reserve de Reverend Corbieres Blanc 1995 13.5 C

Vouvray Lacheteau 1995 15 C

Dry with a very fruity (pear, lemon and peach) fullness which is quite delicious. The perfect garden afternoon wine with the crossword for company.

GERMAN WINE — WHITE

Liebfraumilch, Booths 13 B

Louis Guntrum Niersteiner Bildstock Kerner Beerenauslese 1985 13 G

Piesporter Michelsberg, Booths 13.5 B

GREEK WINE — RED

Vin de Crete Kourtaki 1995 13 B

HUNGARIAN WINE — WHITE

Chapel Hill Oaked Chardonnay, Balaton Boglar NV 15 B

Not a trace of wood, it's all lemon. Thus for sardines, grilled and smoky, this is an utterly divine partner.

Chapel Hill Rheinriesling 1995 13 B

A little unconvincing on the finish.

ITALIAN WINE RED

Barolo Giordano 1992 11 F

Capello di Prete Salento, Candido 14.5 D

Swirling flavours, soft and full but not over-ripe.

Chianti Classico Querciabella 1994 13.5 E

Very expensive for haughty drinkability of reasonably well-ordered fruit and tannin. I just would think twice before I paid a tenner for it.

Ciro Librandi Classico 1994 14 D

Warm, giving, very hot-blooded and Italian, and very, very soft at heart.

Copertino Castiglione 1992 14 C

Ruche di Castagnole del Monferrato 1994 16 F

Highly perfumed, beautifully fruity, gorgeously shaped – this is haute couture wine of great class. It is worth twelve quid just to wallow in its subtle complexities and to revel in the joys of ruche, an obscure grape at the best of times.

Salice Salento Candido 1992 14 D

Sangiovese delle Marche Collezione Bodio 12 B

ITALIAN WINE — WHITE

Frascati Sanantonio 1995 13 C

Trebbiano delle Marche Collezione Bodio 12.5 B

MACEDONIAN WINE — RED

Papaver NV 10 B

Light isn't the word for it.

MOLDOVAN WINE — RED

Kirkwood Cabernet Merlot 1994 14.5 B

NEW ZEALAND WINE — WHITE

Ponder Estate Sauvignon Blanc, Marlborough 1995 13.5 D

Lovely controlled grassy undertones and richness. The finish is, however, spineless.

Villa Maria Private Bin Chardonnay, Gisborne 1995 13.5 D

Highly drinkable but too highly priced.

PORTUGUESE WINE RED

Alta Mesa Tinto Estremadura 1995 15.5 B

Brilliant summer quaffing: soft, slightly rich and flavourful and exceedingly friendly.

Espiga Tinto Estremadura 1995 13 C

Light, almost fruity (but I'm being unkind).

Foral, Douro Tinto Reserva 1994 13.5 B

Food-friendly, dry, touch reluctant to reveal its fruit.

Jose Neiva Estremadura 1994 13 B

Light and cherry-bright.

Vinha Nova Vinho de Mesa 13.5 B

Light with dry undertones. Very pleasant tipple.

PORTUGUESE WINE WHITE

Alta Mesa Estremadura 1995 14 B

Soft and brilliantly priced summer glugging. Real flavour to cope with grilled fish.

Espiga Branco Estremadura 1995

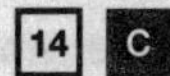

Great flavour and richness here. Excellent food and person wine (i.e. not cooked persons but live conversational ones).

Jose Neiva Estremadura 1994

Real flavour and richness here. Great with chicken and fish.

SOUTH AFRICAN WINE — RED

Capelands Ruby Cabernet, Western Cape 1996

Soft and ripe.

Kumala Cinsault Pinotage 1996

Resounds with rich fruit just like a baked summer pudding set to music (brass section). Big and boisterous.

SOUTH AFRICAN WINE — WHITE

Kumala Colombard/Sauvignon 1996

Welmoed Sauvignon Blanc, Stellenbosch 1996

Mustn't grumble here (label apart). This is a firmly fruity wine of great interest to barbecue pyrotechnicians.

SPANISH WINE RED

Guelbenzu Jardin 1995 15.5 C

Mont Marcal Cabernet Sauvignon, Penedes 1991 14.5 D

Warm, balanced, herby-edged, rich-textured and excellent with anything meaty from a barbecue.

Orobio Tempranillo Rioja 1995 17 C

Very attractive texture, soft, velvety and rolling, and good rich depth of fruit. Lovely summer drink.

Tapas Red 10 B

Vina Alarba, Catalayud 1995 14 B

Touch of sweetness on the finish will help with food if not with glugging.

SPANISH WINE WHITE

Estrella Moscatel de Valencia 16 C

Either with that summer pudding as a dessert wine or as a sweet, floral aperitif, this wine is brilliant. It is summer itself, packed into a bottle.

Rioja Domino de Montalvo Blanco 1994 13.5 D

I find this wine agreeable as it quits the throat but its mode of entry to the mouth is gawky and unconvincing. Okay wine rather than orgasmic for six quid.

Santa Lucia Lightly Oaked Viura, Manchuela 1995  

Superb wine for fishy barbecues and for summer glugging. Full of flavour and style.

Santara Chardonnay, Conca de Barbera 1995  

This is one of the very few chardonnays under four quid which gives Chile a run for the same money: rich, perfectly developed, complex, utterly delicious. It has plot, character and wit. It's a literary gem.

TASMANIAN WINE — WHITE

Ninth Island Chardonnay 1994 14 E

URUGUAYAN WINE — RED

Castol Pujol Tannat 1994  C

Somewhat expensive and not as rampant as previous vintages, but a perfect barbecue bottle.

FORTIFIED WINE

Lustau Old East India Sherry 13.5 E

Fino Sherry, Booths 15 C

SPARKLING WINE/CHAMPAGNE

Barramundi Sparkling (Australia) 15.5 D

Bollinger Grande Anne 1989 9 H

Don't buy this. It's not good enough – and at this price it's obscene. Buy the Deutz from New Zealand – it knocks Bollinger into a cocked chapeau.

Champagne Brut, Booths 14 F

Deutz Marlborough Cuvee (New Zealand) 15.5 E

Considerably more refined and delicately delicious (and well priced) than the champagnes of the same name.

Mont Marcal Gran Reserva 1989 15 E

Here the maturity of the wine is an advantage. It is deep and delicious and very stylish.

Mont Marcal Cava 1992 13 D

Mont Marcal Cava Extra Brut 1989 13 D

An oddity. Rich and very toffee-ish.

Palau Brut (Spain) 14 D

Piper Heidsieck Brut 13 G

Piper Heidsieck Demi Sec 11 F

Prosecco Zonin 14 C

Seaview Rose Brut 15 D

Wonderful summery rose. Quite delicious.

E H Booth & Co Limited
4–6 Fishergate
Preston
Lancs PR1 3LJ
Tel 01772 251701
Fax 01772 204316

Summerplonk 1997

BUDGENS

AUSTRALIAN WINE — RED

Dreamtime Mataro Grenache 1996 12 C

Rather muddy, ill-defined and crude.

AUSTRALIAN WINE — WHITE

Brown Brothers Dry Muscat 1994 13.5 C

Delightful summer afternoon aperitif: light and flowery.

Dreamtime Trebbiano 1996 13.5 C

Dreadful name – the fruit is less so.

Rosemount Estate Hunter Valley Chardonnay 1996 15.5 D

One of the most sublimely elegant and sophisticated of Aussie's chardonnays. Classy stuff.

Rosemount Estate Semillon/Chardonnay 1996 14 D

Balanced, unbashful, excellent with fish.

AUSTRIAN WINE — RED

Blauer Zweigelt 1993

Better than beaujolais for chilled summer drinking – drier too.

BULGARIAN WINE RED

Stara Zagora Vintage Blend Cabernet Sauvignon/Merlot 1994  B

Touch cabbagey on the finish.

BULGARIAN WINE WHITE

Domaine Boyar Vintage Blend Chardonnay/Sauvignon Blanc, Preslav 1995 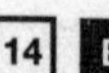

Excellent proposition, both on the pocket and in the glass, for summer fishy barbecues.

Preslav Chardonnay/Sauvignon Blanc 1995  

CHILEAN WINE WHITE

Vina Casablanca Sauvignon Blanc 1996  

Balanced and bonny. Great with barbecued prawns.

Vina Tarapaca Chardonnay 1996 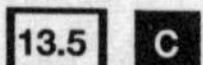

Convincing up front but a touch loose on the finish. I'm wondering if I'm being hypercritical but it is less poised than other '96 Chilean chardonnays.

ENGLISH WINE — WHITE

Lamberhurst High Ridge Fume 1994 7 C

Lamberhurst High Ridge Pink 1994 9 C

FRENCH WINE — RED

Abbaye Saint Hilaire Coteaux Varois 1995 13.5 B

Good herby, characterful fruit of minor earth-moving qualities but extremely drinkable with grilled meats.

Chateau Bassanel Minervois 1995 13 C

Very dry and austere.

Chateau de Malijay Cotes de Rhone 1995 13.5 C

Rhone in the lighter style of roasted earthiness.

Claret 10 B

Costieres de Nimes Fontanilles 1995 14 C

Real earth, clodfuls of it, but great with lamb chops from the barbecue, rich with herbs (the wine is, too).

Cotes du Rhone Villages Cuvee Reserve 1995 12 C

The thin end of the Rhone wedge.

Crozes Hermitage 1994 10 C

Hmm . . . Words fail me . . .

Domaine St Roch VdP de l'Aude 11 B

Faugeres Jean Jean 1994 12 B

Somewhat meagre and a touch constipated.

Le Haut Colombier VdP de la Drome 1995 11 B

Has dryness but not a lot else to its earthiness.

Rouge de France Special Cuvee NV 10 B

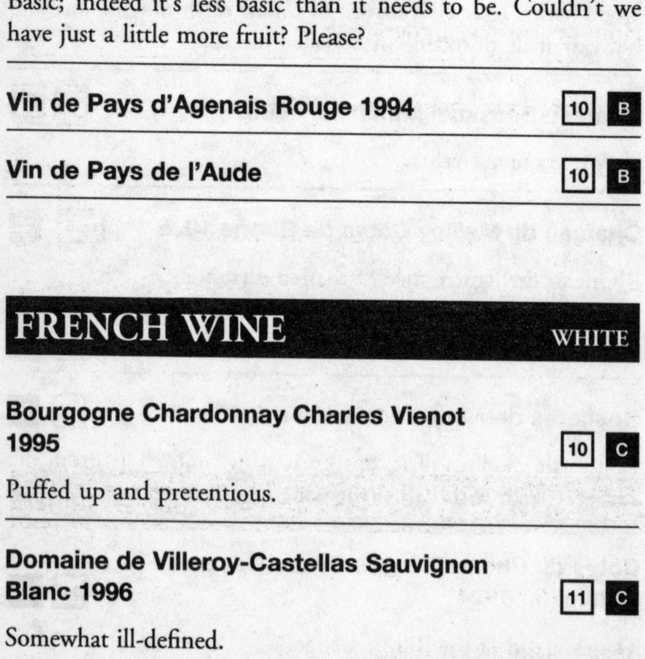

Basic; indeed it's less basic than it needs to be. Couldn't we have just a little more fruit? Please?

Vin de Pays d'Agenais Rouge 1994 10 B

Vin de Pays de l'Aude 10 B

FRENCH WINE WHITE

Bourgogne Chardonnay Charles Vienot 1995 10 C

Puffed up and pretentious.

Domaine de Villeroy-Castellas Sauvignon Blanc 1996 11 C

Somewhat ill-defined.

Domaine l'Argentier Terret VdP des Cotes de Thau 1995 13.5 B

Very faint earthy edge to basic fruit which is not complex but neither is it overwrought.

Domaine Pascaly VdP de l'Aude 12 B

Laroche Grand Cuvee Chardonnay 1995 12 C

Tries hard but really only impressive to the easily impressed and wooden-headed.

Macon Ige 1996 13.5 C

Hints of class – at a price.

Sancerre Les Chasseignes 1994 10 E

Simply very poor value.

Valblanc VdP du Gers Colombard 1995 14.5 B

Fruity, simple, fun, very elegantly bottled (chic isn't the word for it) and excellent summer drinking. Very good value.

GERMAN WINE RED

Dornfelder 1994 11 C

Appley, light, rather thin.

GERMAN WINE — WHITE

Bereich Bernkastel Mosel Saar Ruwer 1995 11 C

Flonheimer Adelberg Auslese 1994 13 C

Sweet? Almost – but on a hot day I enjoy fruit like this (in small doses).

Rudesheimer Rosegarten Gustav Adolf Schmitt, Nahe 1995 10 C

Schmitt von Schmitt Niersteiner Spatlese 1995 13 C

A glass would by no means be despised if the weather was sultry and the company sexy.

HUNGARIAN WINE — RED

Hungarian Cabernet Sauvignon 1994 12 B

HUNGARIAN WINE — WHITE

Hungarian Chardonnay 1993 10 B

ITALIAN WINE RED

Avignonesi Vino Nobile de Montepulciano 1993 12 E

Vastly overpriced for a stylish, dry, highly drinkable wine.

Merlot del Veneto, Ricordi 1995 12 C

Rather vegetal.

Merlot del Veneto Zonin 12 B

ITALIAN WINE WHITE

Colombara Soave Classico, Zenato 1995 15 C

One of the cutest soaves around. Really lives up to its name: a suave, sophisticated, flavoursome, balanced, stylish wine.

Frascati Casale dei Grillo 1995 10 C

A really dull dog of a wine.

NEW ZEALAND WINE RED

Montana Cabernet Sauvignon/Merlot 1995 14.5 D

Grass meets wet earth, but the result, though interesting, is not exactly paydirt. A dry, vegetal wine which needs food.

Waimanu Premium Dry 5 C

Totally disgusting (almost – well, it gets 5).

NEW ZEALAND WINE — WHITE

Waimanu Premium Dry

Somewhat gawky of gait but tries to please – maybe it would be more interesting if it didn't give a damn.

PORTUGUESE WINE — RED

Alta Mesa 1994

Decent summer barbecue stuff (to drink, not to grill) – cheap enough.

Dao Reserve Dom Ferraz 1992

Used to be a cracker, this wine, got sloppy in its old age. Pull your socks up, Dom!!

PORTUGUESE WINE — WHITE

Alta Mesa White 1994

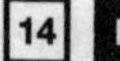

ROMANIAN WINE — WHITE

Tarnava Valley Chardonnay 1995 15 C

I've tasted white burgundies five times more expensive which are less profoundly fruity than this food-friendly bottle. The muscat in the blend is a brilliant sleight of winemaking skilldoggery. *[Ed note: sic.]*

SOUTH AFRICAN WINE — RED

Clear Mountain Pinotage 12.5 C

Warm, soupy, very adolescently fruity.

SOUTH AFRICAN WINE — WHITE

Clear Mountain Chenin Blanc 13.5 B

SPANISH WINE — RED

Diego de Almagro Valdepenas 1993 13.5 B

Amusing label – good to take to a party. The wine inside? Great with burnt sausages.

Marques de Caro Garnacha Reserva 1991

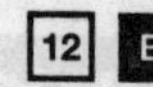

Old-fashioned Spanish gut-swill.

Marques de Caro Merlot 1995

Least leathery merlot I've ever tasted – more like muslin.

SPANISH WINE — WHITE

Chasselas Romand 1996

Has the virtue of being screwcapped, so no nasty tree bark cork to gum up the works. Alas, the fruit in the bottle is a little screwy, too.

USA WINE — RED

E & J Gallo Turning Leaf Zinfandel 1994 12 D

USA WINE — WHITE

E & J Gallo Turning Leaf Chardonnay 1994 14 D

SPARKLING WINE/CHAMPAGNE

Brossault Rose Champagne 13 F

Has some elegance and bite.

Germain Brut Champagne 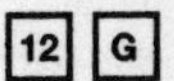

Light, subtly lemonic. But too expensive and not special enough. Cava knocks spots off it.

Budgens Stores Limited
PO Box 9
Stonefield Way
Ruislip
Middlesex HA4 0JR
Tel 0181 422 9511
Fax 0181 422 1596

Summerplonk 1997

CO-OP

ARGENTINIAN WINE RED

Argentine Malbec Sangiovese 1996, Co-op

Has an aromatic pungency reminiscent of strawberry jam and this rich theme is carried through the fruit – except it is dry to finish. An individual, very interesting wine.

Graffigna Shiraz/Cabernet Sauvignon 1995

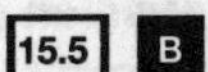

Dry, tobaccoey, rich, deep, characterful – this is an excellent red for anyone's money. A superb barbecue wine.

Lost Pampas Cabernet Malbec 1996

Mission Peak Argentine Red NV

Dry, rather austere.

Weinert Malbec 1991

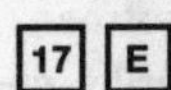

An expensive treat of such mature, tannic richness and lingering muscle-bound fruit that it cries out for food. Great with meat and cheese dishes. The texture is world-class. Puts scores of major bordeaux to shame. At top Co-ops only.

ARGENTINIAN WINE WHITE

Argentine Sauvignon-Torrontes 1996, Co-op

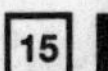

Balbi Syrah Rose 1996 13.5 C

Needs to be well chilled for its richness to shine through. It's certainly a good food wine, fish or meat, but for me it's a mite too cloyingly fruity as a general glugging wine. Only at Co-op Superstores.

Lost Pampas Oak-aged Chardonnay 1996 14 C

Mission Peak Argentine White NV 14.5 B

AUSTRALIAN WINE — RED

Australian Cabernet Sauvignon 1995, Co-op 14.5 C

Unusually brisk, dry Aussie cabernet with developed tannic softness, strength and character. A handsome partner for roasts, grills, cheeses.

Australian Red, Co-op 12 B

Jammy and juicy.

Baileys Shiraz 1994 16 D

Chateau Reynella Cabernet/Merlot 1993 17 D

Jacaranda Hill Grenache 1996, Co-op 14.5 C

Kasbah Shiraz/Malbec/Mourvedre 1993 13 C

Co-op Superstores only.

Kingston Shiraz/Mataro 1995 14.5 C

It has grip and presence, good fruit, firm balance, and it has style, length, flavour and wallop.

Leasingham Domaine Cabernet Malbec 1993 15 E

Lindemans Bin 45 Cabernet Sauvignon 1994 14.5 D

Woodstock Grenache 1995 13 D

Cinnamon toast! Co-op Superstores only.

AUSTRALIAN WINE WHITE

Australian Chardonnay 1996, Co-op 15 C

Brilliant texture and combination of melony fruit and pineapple/ citric acidity. Super summer drinking here.

Australian White, Co-op 14 B

Raw, basic, good lemony edge and attractive value. And very attractive company for fish.

Best's Late Harvest Muscat 1995 14.5 D

Butterfly Ridge Sauvignon Blanc/Chenin Blanc 1996 14 C

The perfect fish barbecue wine. Has a rich, almost cloying depth of clinging flavour and with a mackerel, say, I'd be well satisfied. Only at Co-op Superstores.

Hardys Nottage Hill Chardonnay 1994 17 C

Best vintage yet. Lovely textured, oily fruit, never overdone or blowsy and a buttery, melony finish of surefooted delivery. Terrific value for such classy drinking.

Jacaranda Hill Chenin Verdelho 1996, Co-op 14 C

Kingston Colombard Chardonnay 1995 14 C

Decently fruity with touches of depth to its texture which make it good with food. Only at Co-op Superstores.

Koala Creek Dry White 1996 14 B

Leasingham Domaine Semillon 1993 16 D

Pineapple and lime and gentle undertones to the firmly textured, buttery frontal assault of the fruit which is wonderful with squid dishes – and gently spiced Thai fish dishes. Co-op Superstores only.

Loxton Low Alcohol Chardonnay NV 0 B

Murrumbidgee Estate Fruity Australian White NV 12.5 B

Richmond Grove Verdelho, Cowra Vineyard 1993 15.5 

AUSTRIAN WINE — WHITE

Winzerhaus Gruner Veltliner 1995 13.5 C

BRAZILIAN WINE — RED

Amazon Cabernet Sauvignon 13.5 C

BRAZILIAN WINE — WHITE

Amazon Chardonnay 11 C

BULGARIAN WINE — RED

Bulgarian Vintners' Reserve Cabernet Sauvignon, Rousse 1990 14.5 C

Domaine Boyar Pomorie Cabernet Merlot NV 15 B

As a general summer glug, and party wine, this wine has that added dimension of elegance, richness and dry food-friendliness which will keep people drinking. It is difficult to believe the quality for the money.

Lyaskovets Cabernet Sauvignon 1990 16 B

One of the bargains of the summer. A mature, perfectly weighted, hugely gluggable yet grilled meat-friendly red of class, style, depth and savouriness. The label sucks a bit but you may confidently slurp.

Rousse Cabernet Sauvignon/Cinsault Country Wine 15 B

The Bulgarian Vintners Sliven Merlot/Pinot Noir 14.5 B

Simple slurping with decent fruit. Not much evidence of varietal oomph from the merlot but the pinot nicely pricks the palate. Terrific value.

BULGARIAN WINE WHITE

Domaine Boyar Preslav Chardonnay/Sauvignon Blanc 1996 16 B

Utterly seductive blend of buttery chardonnay with green lime-fruited sauvignon. Superb to glug, to swig with fish, to bathe in – if you've a mind. And at £2.89 you don't need to be obscenely well-heeled. Only at Co-op Superstores.

Lyaskovets Chardonnay 1996 14 B

A rich, well-textured wine of great interest to fish barbecue-ists.

Pomorie Chardonnay Aligote

Delicious crisp simplicity with a hint of sweet ripe melon on the finish.

CHILEAN WINE — RED

Chilean Cabernet Sauvignon, Curico Valley, Co-op

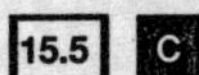

What polish! What hauteur! For grace, flavour, texture and effortless smoothness for the money, this is good enough to be the house red wine at a Michelin 3-star restaurant.

Four Rivers Cabernet Sauvignon 1995

Another fantastic Co-op bargain. This is no run-of-the-mill cabernet (although it has classic touches of pepper) for there is an immense flourish of bright brambly fruit on the finish. A lovely sustaining glug.

La Fortuna Malbec 1996

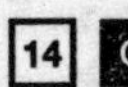

Rich, very dry, characterful and gently rustic. But it will improve over the next twenty months and rate maybe 16 points or more in time. Co-op Superstores only.

Long Slim Cabernet/Merlot 1994

Improving considerably in bottle, this wine oozes class, depth, flavour, terrific fruit and tannic balance and a lingering presence of wines twice the price.

Santa Carolina Merlot 1994 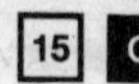

Tierra del Rey Chilean Red NV 

Fantabulous for the dosh. Has good evolved tannins, excellent depth of fruit with alert acidity, and a decent finish of no-hurry-to-quit demeanour. It is immensely drinkable, likeable, charming and good with food.

CHILEAN WINE — WHITE

Caliterra Casablanca Chardonnay 1994 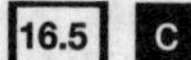

Superb rich edge to the final thrust of the elegant fruit. Impressive wine with gusto, flavour and real style.

Four Rivers Chardonnay 1996 

Loose and a touch gauche but it will perform well with food (even if at £3.99 it is rather outclassed by many other Chileans).

Long Slim White Chardonnay/Semillon 1996 

It has a blowsy richness of depth but this isn't entirely disreputable for the mannered acidity on the finish turns a louche wine charming – if rather brassy to begin.

Santa Carolina Chardonnay 1996  

I love this wine. It is so well-flavoured, rich yet never overblown, stylishly balanced and really convincingly textured. Loads of class here. Only at Co-op Superstores and Supermarkets.

Tierra del Rey Chilean White NV 

Utterly delicious, rich-edged fruit of style and flavour. A cracking companion to fish, poultry, salads and animated, food-less conversation.

Vina Casablanca Sauvignon Blanc 1996 

One of the most elegant sauvignons around: stylish, prim, quietly rich, fresh and beautifully well-textured. Only at Co-op Superstores.

CHINESE WINE RED

Dragon Seal Cabernet Sauvignon 1993 

CHINESE WINE WHITE

Dragon Seal Chardonnay 1993 14 

ENGLISH WINE WHITE

Denbies English Table Wine 1992 

C

FRENCH WINE RED

Bad Tempered Cyril Tempranillo/Syrah NV 14 C

The label alone is worth giving to a wine snob. The fruit is simple, bright, soft with a hint of earthy dryness, and very drinkable. Good summer wine.

Barton & Guestier Margaux Tradition 1992 13 E

Beaujolais Villages Domaine Granjean 1995 12 C

Soft and drinkable but why pay a fiver for it when the Co-op has such brilliant £2.99 wines of greater fruity excitement? Only at Co-op Superstores.

Bergerac Rouge, Co-op 12 B

Somewhat dry and austere, but okay with food.

Cabernet Sauvignon VdP d'Oc, Co-op 13 B

Rather dry and austere.

Cahors, Co-op 12 C

Dry, reluctant to enchant. Only at Co-op Superstores.

Chateau Cissac 1986 11 F

Chateau Fourtanet 1993 14.5 D

Classic dryness from Castillon with superb compatibility with roast meats. Co-op Superstores only.

Chateau Pierrousselle Bordeaux 1996 14 C

A terrific little bordeaux for the money with rich, deep tannins. Great with barbecued meats. The suppleness of the fruit nicely accompanies these tannins.

Claret, Co-op 12 B

Cotes de Beaune Villages Jules Vignon 1995 10 D

Cotes du Luberon, Co-op 11 B

Only at Co-op Superstores.

Cotes du Rhone, Co-op 13 B

Very attractive, inky red. Not a deal of complexity and it isn't typically earthy.

Cotes du Roussillon, Co-op 15 B

Cotes du Ventoux, Co-op 14 B

Crozes Hermitage Louis Mousset 1994 13.5 C

Domaine de Conquet Merlot 1994 14 C

Has dryness and a certain richness which show their best with rich grilled vegetables and meats.

Fitou, Co-op 13 C

Decent enough – with good earthy fruit and appealing tannins.

Fleurie, Mommessin 1995 12.5 D

Hardys Bordeaux Rouge 1995 13.5 C

An Aussie's idea of Bordeaux. It isn't the classicist's. Co-op Superstores only.

Medoc Vieilles Vignes 1993 10 C

Stringy and gawky.

Meffre Oak-Aged Cotes du Rhone 1995 14 C

Real weight of teeth-gripping fruit which is rather juicy, curiously, on the finish. Co-op Superstores only.

Merlot VdP d'Oc, Co-op 14 B

Dry, somewhat restrained on the warmth it radiates, but thoroughly satisfying (and well priced) with bangers and mash.

Morgon, Les Charmes 1994 13.5 D

Moulin a Vent Pierre Leduc 1995 13 D

Quite classy in its own way (i.e. beaujolais). But pricey. Only at Co-op Superstores.

Nuits St Georges, Pierre Leduc 1994 10 E

Dull and pricey. I'd rather drink Cola. Only at Co-op Superstores.

Oak-Aged Claret, Co-op 13.5 C

Oak-Aged Cotes du Rhone 1995, Co-op 13.5 C

Pommard, Pierre Leduc 1994 10 F

Boring and expensive. Only a clot buys a wine like this at this price. Only at Co-op Superstores.

St Emilion, Bernard Taillan (half bottle) 13 C

Valreas Domaine de la Grande Bellane 1995 (Organic) 14.5 D

An organic, vegetarian wine – a rare double appeal of ethics and ecological extremity – and it is very, very drinkable. It is a touch smug and pleased with itself, even mannerly, but as it is so easy to like it isn't earthy and bad-tempered. Only at Co-op Superstores.

Vin de Pays d'Oc Cabernet Merlot 14 C

A very cherry/plum wine of simplicity, charm and direct drinkability. Hasn't the robustness to counterpunch with rich food, but it's an attractive mouthful, chilled too. Only at Co-op Superstores.

Vin de Pays de l'Aude, Co-op 10 B

Vin de Pays de l'Herault Rouge, Co-op 14 B

Very, very friendly. Dry and warm wine with a juicy touch on the finish.

Winter Hill Red 1995 15 B

FRENCH WINE WHITE

Alsace Gewurztraminer 1995 15.5 C

What a treat for the summer! It's difficult to think of a more delicious start to an evening or with a Thai take-away. It's spicy, roseate, utterly delicious. Only at Co-op Superstores and Supermarkets.

Bergerac Blanc, Co-op 11 B

Chablis, Les Vignerons de Chablis 1995 12 E

Drinkable but frightfully expensive.

Chateau la Jaubertie Bergerac Blanc 1995 14.5 C

Rich, well-textured, rather more flat than Bergeracs normally are but this is all to the good. A plump, English-inspired wine.

Chateau Pierrousselle Entre Deux Mers 1996 14.5 C

Quietly classy. Doesn't mess about trying to be something it isn't. It's simply a good shellfish wine.

Domaine de Haut Rauly Monbazillac 1994 (half bottle) 14.5 C

Fair Martina Vermentino NV 14.5 C

Fleur du Moulin Chardonnay VdP d'Oc 1996 13.5 C

Light, floral, peachy – a simple glugging chardonnay of easy-going charm.

Hermitage Blanc, Les Nobles Rives 1992 13 F

Le Galet Reserve Chardonnay, VdP d'Oc 1995 13 D

Rather overpriced. Co-op Superstores only.

Les Pavois d'Or, Sauternes (half bottle) 13 D

Montagny Premier Cru 1995 11 D

Philippe de Baudin Chardonnay 1994 15 C

Premieres Cotes de Bordeaux, Co-op 13 C

Rose d'Anjou, Co-op 13.5 B

A delicate but assertive rose, good with all sorts of food. Most attractive barbecue wine.

Sauvignon Blanc Bordeaux, Co-op 13 B

VdP d'Oc Chardonnay, Co-op 12 C

VdP de l'Herault Blush, Co-op 11 C

Vin de Pays de Vaucluse Chardonnay/ Viognier NV  15.5 B

Fabulous well-ordered marriage of grapes and a real steal at the price. Terrific breadth to the fruit, to the texture, to the balance and to the finish – everywhere, in fact, except the price tag. A non-vintage wine but it is all fresh '96 juice. Only at Co-op Superstores.

Vin de Pays des Cotes de Gascogne, Co-op 13.5 B

Excellent tipple for a warm summer evening or afternoon in the back garden. Chill it well.

Vin de Pays des Cotes des Pyrenees Orientales NV, Co-op 14 B

Perfect little barbecue companion. Has a lilting drinkability.

Viognier VdP d'Oc 1994 13 C

Winter Hill White 1995 13.5 B

GERMAN WINE RED

Dornfelder, Co-op 13 C

GERMAN WINE WHITE

Bad Bergzaberner Kloster Liebfrauenberg Auslese 1994 15 C

Forster Schnepfenflug Riesling Kabinett 1995 12 C

Co-op Superstores only.

Graacher Himmelreich Riesling Spatlese 1994 14 C

Treat with respect. Yes, the fruit is off-dry and ripe but there's some lovely sherbety acidity, deliciously citric, and this makes the wine a superb warm day, back garden aperitif. I love a glass or two in these circumstances. Only at Co-op Superstores and Supermarkets.

Morio Muskat, Co-op 12.5 B

Muller Thurgau, Co-op 12 B

Rudesheimer Rosengarten 1994, Co-op 13 B

GREEK WINE RED

Vin de Crete Red, Kourtaki 1995 13 B

HUNGARIAN WINE RED

Chapel Hill Cabernet Sauvignon, Balaton 1994 13.5 B

Very pleasant but it's lost its bite at three years old.

Hungarian Red, Co-op 13 B

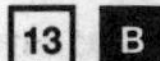

Very quiet, reserved, cherry-ripe and slips down easily.

Hungaroo Merlot 1995 14 B

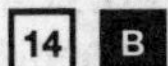

Dry, chewy, cherry/plum fruit of firm stylishness.

HUNGARIAN WINE WHITE

Chapel Hill Irsai Oliver 1995 15 B

Hungarian White, Co-op 14.5 B

Terrific lemon edge to convincing up-front fruit of charm and style. Drink it on its own or with food – it's willing to please on all fronts.

Hungaroo Pinot Gris 1995 15 B

Hungaroo Sauvignon Blanc 1995 14 C

Faintly reminiscent of Kiwi sauvignon in its initial grassiness. An excellent shellfish stew wine – really good value.

ITALIAN WINE RED

Bardolino Le Canne, Boscaini 1995 13.5 C

Lightly fruity, cherries sprinkled on plums. Only at Co-op Superstores.

Chianti 1995, Co-op 12 C

Very light and terribly uncompetitive.

Chianti Classico, Otto Santi 1994 12 D

Co-op Superstores only.

Country Collection Puglian Red 15.5 B

Le Volte Ornellaia 1993 12 E

Merlot del Veneto, Co-op 12.5 C

Monferrato Rosso 13.5 B

Flops all over the tastebuds like a big bumbling puppy dog.

Montepulciano d'Abruzzo 1994, Co-op 13.5 B

Principato Rosso, Co-op 12 B

Sangiovese di Toscana, Fiordaliso 1994 15 C

Sicilian Red, Co-op 12 B

Almost sweet in its fruitiness. Good with meat and vegetable curries and Balti dishes.

Torresolada Sicilian Red 1995 11 B

Valpolicella, Co-op 13 B

Light, and doesn't hurt the throat. But equally doesn't set the tastebuds alight.

Valpolicella Marano, Boscaini 1995 12 C

Straightforward – a square peg in a square hole. How cosy and dull can you get? Only at Co-op Superstores.

Villa Mantinera, Montepulciano de Molise NV 14 C

Vino da Tavola Rosso NV, Co-op 10 B

Sweet and juicy.

ITALIAN WINE WHITE

Alasia Chardonnay del Piemonte 1995 14 C

Bianco di Custoza Vignagrande 1995 10 C

Co-op Superstores only.

Chardonnay Atesino, Co-op 10 B

Chardonnay del Salento, 'Le Trulle' 1994 15.5 C

Frascati Superiore 1995, Co-op 12 C

Dull, and a touch mawkish.

Frascati Villa Catone 1994 11 C

Monferrato Bianco 13 B

Orvieto Secco, Co-op 11 C

Unthrilling and overpriced.

Pinot Grigio del Veneto, Co-op 10 B

Principato Valdadige 1995 13.5 B

Good solid fresh fruit.

Sicilian White, Co-op 13 B

Soave, Co-op 12 B

Dullish.

Soave Monteleone, Boscaini 1996 14 C

One of the most elegant soaves around: rich, balanced, very finely flavoured. Only at Co-op Superstores.

Torresolada Bianco di Sicilia 1995 14.5 B

Sunny label, sunny disposition. Handsome partner for fish and for general glugging. Only at Co-op Superstores.

Vino da Tavola Bianco NV, Co-op 11 B

LEBANESE WINE RED

Chateau Musar 1977 13 G

Chateau Musar 1988 13 G

MACEDONIAN WINE RED

Macedonian Vranac/Cabernet Sauvignon 1993  B

Not at all bad, considering how it has been in the past. It's dry, rich, decently fruity in a quiet cabernet manner, and it is easy to drink. Only at Co-op Superstores and Supermarkets.

MEXICAN WINE RED

L A Cetto Petite Syrah 1993 16 C

Wonderful texture and weighted richness of fruit.

MOLDOVAN WINE RED

Kirkwood Cabernet Merlot 1994 11 

Rapidly losing its personality and bite.

MOLDOVAN WINE WHITE

Kirkwood Chardonnay 1995 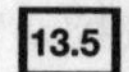

Getting to the end of its shelf-life, this fruit, but still fair value.

MOROCCAN WINE RED

Moroccan Cabernet Sauvignon/Syrah 1995  B

NEW ZEALAND WINE RED

New Zealand Cabernet Merlot 1994, Co-op  

NEW ZEALAND WINE — WHITE

Forest Flower Fruity Dry White 1995 13.5 C

Millton Vineyard Semillon/Chardonnay 1995 12 D

New Zealand Semillon Sauvignon Blanc 1995, Co-op 14.5 C

Nobilo White Cloud 1995 13 C

PORTUGUESE WINE — RED

Campos dos Frades Cabernet Sauvignon 1995 15 C

Smoky, rich, tobacco-scented, deep, dry, full of flavour and very gripping. Excellent value.

Duque de Viseu Dao 1992 13 D

Somewhat austere. Co-op Superstores only.

Quinta da Pancas Cabernet Sauvignon 1995 16 D

This vintage demonstrates this purposeful estate's commitment to really stylish, warm, complex cabernets without a hint of coarseness. Great tannins, superb fruit, lovely balance and all-round compactness.

Quinta da Pancas Cabernet Sauvignon 1994 16 D

A delicious cabernet of elegance and style, improving nicely in bottle. Has richness and cabernet dryness but a complex woody undertone intrudes delightfully into the rich fruit adding a savoury note. It's a hugely gluggable wine of class and excellent with light meats – lamb especially. Only at Co-op Superstores.

Ramada, Estremadura 1994 14.5 B

A simple fruit glug? Not a flawed notion but . . . what about the hot sunny edge to the fruit? What about the smoothness? What about the sheer pleasure of it?

Star Mountain Oak Aged Touriiga 1994 14 C

Very individual. Dry, earthy, quaintly exotically edged (spicy ripe figs), and immensely capable of handling rich meat and veg dishes. Only at Co-op Superstores and Supermarkets.

Vila Santa 1995 15.5 D

A lovely, rich, textured wine of superbly smooth yet dry, cassis-edged fruitiness. It is classy in a home-spun way, deep, savoury, with a hint of jam, and very, very drinkable. It has an invigorating healthy kick to it. Only at Co-op Superstores.

PORTUGUESE WINE WHITE

Campos dos Frades Chardonnay 1995 14.5 C

Most attractive as it hits the nostrils where a classic richness hints at a wine of greater finesse than one would have thought possible from Portugal. The fruit is more down to earth – but still attractive. Co-op Superstores only.

Fiuza Sauvignon Blanc 1995 16 C

A brilliantly conceived wine of striking, balanced fruit. Richness and style in abundance.

Joao Pires Muscat Branco 1995 15.5 C

Vinho Verde, Co-op 12 B

But . . . but . . . on a hot day a glass of this spritzig, spineless gunk is most pleasant. A glass, mind you, no more.

ROMANIAN WINE RED

Classic Pinot Noir 1991 16 B

Mature yet lithe, soft, fruity, complex and, incredibly, a proper gamy pinot. Great value.

River Route Merlot 1995 16 B

Brilliant merlot: rich, aromatic, good development of fruit with the tannins, this is good with food, highly drinkable without. Staggeringly good value.

Romanian Country Red 14.5 B

Curious, polished fruit with a flavour of baked plum. Lovely drinkability here.

Romanian Prairie Merlot 1995, Co-op 13 B

Special Reserve Merlot, Sahateni Barrel-matured 1994 17 C

A perfect balance of rich, savoury, leather-edged fruit of

astonishing texture, evolved tannins, and style and excellent acidity. This is a remarkable wine for under a fiver. The polish, the quality of fruit, the layers of flavour are all on song and deeply impressive. Only at Co-op Superstores.

ROMANIAN WINE — WHITE

River Route Sauvignon Blanc 1995 13.5 B

Good with shellfish. Needs food.

Romanian Country White 11 C

Romanian Prairie Sauvignon Blanc 1995, Co-op 15 B

SOUTH AFRICAN WINE — RED

Cape Afrika Pinotage 1992 14 C

A cheroot-edged wine of depth, dryness and richness – a touch expensive – but delicious with barbecued meats and sausages. Only at Co-op Superstores and Supermarkets.

Cape Red, Co-op 14.5 B

Perfectly priced, perfectly balanced red of positive charms: fruity (but no burnt rubber), good depth of flavour counterpointed in its savoury soupiness by zest acidity.

Jacana Merlot, Hugh Ryman 1995 14.5 D

Rather classy if somewhat rich in tannins which will soften and improve over the next eighteen months in bottle. But there is no gainsaying the rich quality of the fruit or the positive ambitions of the winemaker. Co-op Superstores only.

Kumala Cinsault/Pinotage 16 B

Burnt rubber fruit of great charm. Distinctive, soft, deliciously well-formed and stylish! Exceptional depth of flavour and lingering-finished fruitiness.

Kumala Shiraz/Cabernet Sauvignon 1996 

This is rather young and feisty at the moment – it needs a few more months in bottle to develop greater couthness. However, it still rates well for it has a briskness which is not entirely bereft of charm.

Long Mountain Shiraz 1993 15 C

Oak Village Cabernet Sauvignon 1992 13.5 C

Oak Village Pinotage 1995 14.5 C

Delicious charcoal-edged richness balanced by a flavoursome acidic zip. Great pasta wine.

Robertson Cabernet Sauvignon 1994 14.5 C

Robertson Merlot 1996 14 C

A light merlot of some style, with cherry/plum fruit of standard drinkability, and an easy, relaxed texture. Not deep or complex, it is, nevertheless, hard to dislike. Only at Co-op Superstores.

SOUTH AFRICAN WINE WHITE

Cape Afrika Rhine Riesling 1996

C

Touch of waxy, off-dry honey to the melony fruit makes it a great warm-weather glug. Only at Co-op Superstores and Supermarkets.

Cape White, Co-op

B

Somewhat less appealing than once it was. Has age withered its freshness?

Goudini Chardonnay 1996

Tasty, warm, not overstraining itself or blowsy and overrich. But it does have depth and style. Co-op Superstores only.

Kumala Chenin/Chardonnay 1995

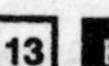

B

Oak Village Chardonnay 1995

C

Olive Grove Chardonnay 1996

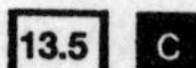

The finish is quirky, and spoils the effect for me, but I am being very critical (and this wine is £4.50). The initial fruit attack is fine, though. Only at Co-op Superstores.

Overgaauw Chardonnay 1995

A lovely, layered, rich, harmonious, delicious wine of considerable flair and wit. The wood and fruit are in perfect step, giving a creamy richness, and the finish is textured and bright. Co-op Superstores only.

Welmoed Sauvignon Blanc 1996

Elegant, gentle but with fleshy hints of rich fruit aromatically and on the finish. Co-op Superstores only.

SPANISH WINE — RED

Berberana Tempranillo Rioja 1995

Needs food, I reckon, to nullify the rather ripe finish. But in approach its fruit is fleshy and attractively perfumed.

Campo Rojo, Carinena

Enate Tempranillo Cabernet 1992

Aromatic, smooth, classy, well-mannered. It's perhaps almost TOO smooth and classy for its rustic background. It has the politeness perhaps to be expected from a wine made by a man who worked at Chateau Margaux and Torres.

Gandia Cabernet Sauvignon 1993

Rather austere and costive. Doesn't give much, but is impressively distant.

Gandia Cabernet Sauvignon 1995

Only just rates 14. It sneaks in by virtue of its frontal attack of dry fruit, but the finish is a touch ho-hum.

Marino Tinto NV

Has a delicious (though simple) dry jamminess.

Marques de la Sierra Garnacha 1994 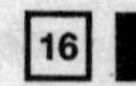

Brilliant value and simply terrific with casseroles and roasts. Has a good shroud of dry, rich tannin and an undercoat of soft berry fruit. Lovely texture, solid fruit with a hint of spice. It has a concentration of flavour and complexity which is stunning for the money.

Marquis de Monistrol Merlot 1993 

Has a lovely warmth to its fruit allied to a soft developed texture of decent interwoven flavours – mainly plum. Only at Co-op Superstores and Supermarkets.

Palacio de la Vega Cabernet Sauvignon 1992 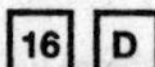

Texture, warmth, richness, style, humour and personality. Dry yet full of fruit.

Rioja Tinto NV, Co-op 

You can spread this thickly on dry toast and chew with great satisfaction. Has depth, flavour, class, modern Riojan richness and lovely texture.

Santara Cabernet/Merlot, Conca de Barbera 1994 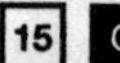

Delicious union of grapes, a perfect sum of parts, offering richness, depth and texture. A classy feel to the wine is granted by this texture which confers on the fruit a lovely meatiness. Only at Co-op Superstores and Supermarkets.

Tempranillo Oak-Aged, Co-op 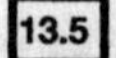 

Torres Gran Sangredetoro 1989 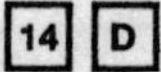

Vina Pomal Rioja Crianza 1990 13.5 C

SPANISH WINE — WHITE

Berberana Carta de Oro 1995 13 C

Very attractive with a fish, where I'd rate it 14.5, but as a glug it takes some taste acquiring. Only at Co-op Superstores and Supermarkets.

Castillo de Monjardin Chardonnay 1995 

The '95 vintage of this wine is somewhat muted at the moment. Little presence aromatically, fruit on the acidic side rather than mellow – but it will improve over a year in bottle. Co-op Superstores only.

Castillo de Monjardin Unoaked Chardonnay 1994 14.5 C

Gandia Chardonnay Hoya Valley 1994 15.5 C

A buttery version of chardonnay with a limpid, subtle citricity. Delicious fruit.

Gandia Hoya Valley Grenache Rose 1995 13 C

Adolescent, infuriatingly fruity and eager to please but on a hot summer day it would be fab (darling).

Santara Chardonnay 1995 16.5 C

This is one of the very few chardonnays under four quid which gives Chile a run for the same money: rich, perfectly developed, complex, utterly delicious. It has plot, character and wit. It's a literary gem. Co-op Superstores only.

Torres Sangredetoro 1992 12 C

Valle de Monterrey Dry White Wine, Co-op 13 B

USA WINE RED

Beringer Zinfandel 1992 14 D

California Red, Co-op 13.5 B

A pleasant, peasant alternative to beaujolais, chianti and valpolicella.

Gallo Sonoma County Cabernet Sauvignon 1992 14 E

Glen Ellen Merlot 1994 15 C

Hedges Cabernet Sauvignon/Merlot, Columbia 1994 15.5 E

Better than many a vaunted claret at three times the price. The fruit and tannin stride out together with purpose and style and show a real turn of delicacy yet weight on the tastebuds. A very classy wine. Co-op Superstores only.

Redwood Trail Pinot Noir 1995 14 D

Has true pinot aroma, truffle and warm, and a decent thwack of farmyardy wild raspberry-edged fruit. Better, much better, than the Co-op red burgundies at twice the price. Only at Co-op Superstores.

USA WINE — WHITE

Arbor Crest Chardonnay 1995 14 E

Richness, depth, flavour and fullness. Very classy, very expensive, very all-embracing American. Only at Co-op Superstores.

California Colombard, Co-op 13 B

Only at Co-op Superstores and Supermarkets.

Glen Ellen Proprietor's Reserve Chardonnay 1995 16 C

Developing more vegetality as it ages but still a richly textured, plump chardonnay of flavour, depth and real engaging fruitiness. It offers a lovely glass of wine to all the senses.

Hedges Fume Chardonnay, Columbia 1995 12 D

Expensive, ill-balanced, and only a force to reckon with at £3.29. Co-op Superstores only.

Sebastiani's White Zinfandel 1995 10 C

Stowells of Chelsea California Blush (3-litre box) 12.5 F

SPARKLING WINE/CHAMPAGNE

Barramundi Sparkling (Australia) 15.5 D

Brown Bros Pinot Noir/Chardonnay NV 14.5 E

Terribly posh feel to this wine. Better than scores of champagnes. Only at Co-op Superstores.

Cava, Co-op  C

Codorniu Premiere Cuvee Brut (Spain) 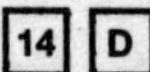

Marino Cava del Mediterraneo  C

An absolute block-buster of a bottle: delicate, lemony, classically fresh, clean and elegant and just so ridiculously well-priced it makes you think twice and drink time and time again (and at £3.99 a bottle you can afford it).

Moscato Spumante, Co-op  

Sweet as a kitten but nowhere near as hairy. The richness is not cloying and a glass is the perfect hot-day start to the day – with the morning papers in the back garden.

Sparkling Saumur, Co-op 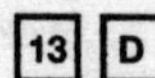

Veuve Honorain Blanc de Noirs Champagne NV 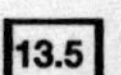 

An elegant bubbly of dry fruitiness – perhaps not as lemonic as it might be.

Co-operative Wholesale Society Limited
PO Box 53
New Century House
Manchester M60 4ES
Tel 0161 834 1212
Fax 0161 834 4507

KWIK SAVE

ARGENTINIAN WINE RED

Balbi Vineyard Malbec Syrah 1995  13 B

AUSTRALIAN WINE RED

Pelican Bay Australian Red Wine NV 14.5 B

Soft, slightly soupy, but good chilled or at back garden temperature with loads of foods and different moods.

Pelican Bay Shiraz Cabernet 1996 13.5 B

AUSTRALIAN WINE WHITE

Pelican Bay Chardonnay 1996 14.5 B

Pelican Bay Medium Dry White 12 B

South Eastern Australia Colombard Chardonnay NV 14 B

Ripe, very fruity, excellent tropical weather thirst-quencher.

BULGARIAN WINE RED

Domaine Boyar Lovico Suhindol Cabernet Sauvignon/Merlot Country Wine 13 B 

BULGARIAN WINE WHITE

Khan Krum Riesling-Dimiat 14 A

Preslav Vintage Blend Chardonnay/ Sauvignon 1995 14 B

CHILEAN WINE RED

Deep Pacific Merlot Cabernet Sauvignon, Rancagua Region 1996 15 B 

Serious cabernet vegetality and peppery capiscum edge may deter the tender-tongued but it opens up deeply fruity and rich on the finish. Terrific for the money.

CHILEAN WINE — WHITE

White Pacific Sauvignon Chardonnay, Rancagua Region 1996

B

Brilliant value for such elegance and demure fruitiness. Has style, balance, subtle flavour and real class.

ENGLISH WINE — WHITE

Denbies 95

B

Excellent fish-and-chip wine. Good price; reasonable crisp fruit.

FRENCH WINE — RED

Cabernet Sauvignon VdP d'Oc 1995

Soft cherries and juicy blackcurrant fruit immediately strike but then the tannins' beautiful return stroke as a back taste gives the wine depth, character, style and brilliant value for money.

Les Oliviers

A pleasant cherry-fruited, cherry-cheeked wine of light appeal.

Rouge de France, Selection Cuvee VE 12 B

Skylark Hill Merlot, VdP d'Oc 15.5 B

Skylark Hill Very Special Red VdP d'Oc 15 B

Gentle rubbery undertone to the fruit which is compact and well presented. Excellent balance of fruit, acid and acidity. A really attractive quaffing wine.

FRENCH WINE WHITE

Blanc de France Vin de Table Selection Cuvee 13 B

Les Oliviers 12 A

Basic: not to say what some would call 'cooking wine'.

Rose de France Selection Cuvee VE 12 B

Skylark Hill Chardonnay VdP d'Oc 14.5 B

Skylark Hill Very Special White, VdP d'Oc 13.5 B

Lemon-edged fruit useful to barbecue fish eaters.

Stowells of Chelsea Vin de Pays du Tarn (3-litre box) 12 F

GERMAN WINE — WHITE

Piesporter Michelsberg, K Linden 1996 13.5 

Try it chilled, just a glass or two, out in the garden in a deckchair with a book or the papers or just the cat on your lap. Now – don't you feel better already?

GREEK WINE — RED

Mavrodaphne of Patras NV 13 

A wine for unseasonal slices of cake, e.g. of the Christmas variety.

GREEK WINE — WHITE

Kourtakis Retsina NV 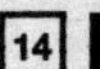 14 

I love retsina. It's a brilliant barbecue fish wine. This one is oily and cricket-bat flavoured.

ITALIAN WINE — RED

Valpolicella Venier 11 

ITALIAN WINE — WHITE

Soave Venier 11 B

SOUTH AFRICAN WINE — RED

Impala Cape Red 1996 14.5 B

Chill it (for fish), throw it at barbecued sausages, pour it out (chilled) for your guests – this wine aims to please.

Impala Pinotage, Western Cape 1996 14 C

Good, rich, gentle fruit which turns satisfyingly vibrant and savoury on the finish.

SOUTH AFRICAN WINE — WHITE

Impala Cape White 1996 13.5 B

Curious wine: it turns all lovey-dovey on the finish. A glass makes a pleasant warm-weather tipple, though.

Impala Chenin Chardonnay 1996 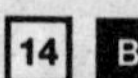

Good nutty fruit on the finish is the final emphasis of a dry, charmingly constructed wine.

Jade Peaks Chenin Blanc 1996 14.5 B

Crisp, melony, hints of mineral acidity, this is an excellent barbecue fish wine and general back-garden quaffer.

SPANISH WINE RED

Flamenco Spanish Full Red 10 B

SPANISH WINE WHITE

Castillo de Liria Moscatel, Valencia 15.5 B

USA WINE RED

California Cellars Red 11 B

USA WINE WHITE

California Cellars White 13 B

SPARKLING WINE/CHAMPAGNE

Bonnet Brut Heritage Champagne 12 F

Champagne Brut, Louis Raymond 13.5 E

Kwik Save Stores Limited
Warren Drive
Prestatyn
Clwyd LL19 7HU
Tel 01745 887111
Fax 01745 882504

Summerplonk 1997

MARKS & SPENCER

ARGENTINIAN WINE RED

Oak Aged Mendoza Malbec 1992 15 D

Has hints of melted chocolate to its dry, rich fruitiness. A mature wine, it needs food.

AUSTRALIAN WINE RED

McLaren Vale Cabernet Sauvignon 1994

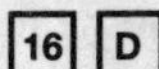

Beautiful example of McLaren Vale fruit: herby, soft, rich, aromatic, smooth yet with lots of flavour and a discreet, well-mannered personality.

Pheasant Gully Riverina Shiraz

Rose Label Orange Vineyard Cabernet Sauvignon, Rosemount Estate 1993

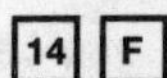

The perfume of spiced plums with ripe fruit to match. The tannins seem detached from this middle-of-the-palate presence and only strike as the wine disappears, most deliciously, down the gullet. It won't get any better with age, so it must be drunk now. But it is very expensive.

Rosemount Estate Shiraz 1994

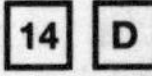

South East Australian Shiraz 1995

Rich, ripe and soft but with enough tannins to keep from going soppy and gooey. Puppyish, yes, but it can be brought to heel and go well with food.

AUSTRALIAN WINE WHITE

Australian Medium Dry, South Eastern Australia 13.5 C

If it gets Gran off Lieb then it's worth the extra quid.

Honey Tree Semillon Chardonnay, Rosemount Estate 1996 15 D

A delicate sipping wine of opulent texture, mild perfume, discreet fruit, fine balance and gentle, soothing manner. Not a bottle for rich food, it makes for refined tippling nevertheless.

Lindemans Bin 65 Chardonnay 1996 15.5 C

Elegant, purposeful, balanced, finely wrought and handsomely textured. A textbook Aussie chardonnay.

Pheasant Gully Colombard Chardonnay 12.5 C

Rose Label Orange Vineyard Chardonnay, Rosemount 1995 16.5 F

Beguiling perfume of woodsmoke and baked croissant, fruit which is both ripe and gently textured (ogen melon with a hint of fig and nuts) and a somewhat discreet finish of gentility and charm. An expensive treat which needs a fully alert and studious palate to catch every nuance. Robust food will kill it. Smoked salmon or grilled fish will enhance it.

Rosemount Estate Chardonnay, Hunter Valley 1995 16 D

Flourish of woody fruit on the finish of a balanced, delicate wine provides delicious compensation for seven quid.

South East Australian Lightly Oaked Chardonnay 1996

C

Lovely, rich oily texture, well-buttered flavour of deep, satisfying, handsomely poised fruitiness which somehow manages to be never less than calm, unfussy and very stylish. A most unusually elegant Aussie chardonnay.

South East Australian Semillon/ Chardonnay

BULGARIAN WINE — RED

Vintners Cabernet Sauvignon, Svischtov 1992

Very ripe and soft for such a comparatively middle-aged wine. I suspect it's past its best.

CHILEAN WINE — RED

Carmen Reserve Merlot 1995

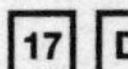

Magnificence for little money: superb fruit of great elegance, floral and fruit complexity (herbs, violets, plums and raspberries) and caressing texture.

Carmen Vineyards Cabernet Sauvignon Reserve 1995

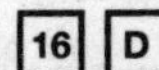

Texturally fruity, aromatically all a delight. Somewhat coy, so robust food is out, but an elegant delight.

Carmen Vineyards Central Valley Cabernet Sauvignon 1994 14 C

Carmen Vineyards Central Valley Merlot 1995 16.5 C

Packed with flavour – like a jamjar crammed to the brim with soft rich fruit – but has depth, character, style, aplomb and a rousing finish. A strikingly savoury wine of polish and texture – the essence of leather-soft, luxuriously appointed merlot.

Carmen Vineyards Maipo Cabernet Sauvignon Reserve 1995 16.5 D

Chocolatey, raspberryish, dry yet full of rounded fruit flavours, great tannic balance, superbly textured and perfectly weighted to go from nose to throat with insidious ease. A lovely wine.

Casa Leona Cabernet Sauvignon 1995 15 C

Brilliant soft, gentle fruit with a brushed-suede edge of finesse.

Casa Leona Merlot 1996 16 C

Soft, aromatic like old club chairs, dark cherry fruit, very vivid, beautifully textured and richly finished.

CHILEAN WINE WHITE

Carmen Vineyards Gewurztraminer Sauvignon 1996 15 D

Spicy and daft, irreverent, full of flavour – great with oriental food and giving to stick-in-the-muds: 'My God! What is this yummy confection?!'

Casa Leona Chardonnay 1996 13.5 C

Lontue Chardonnay 1996 15 C

Quiet, demure, delicate, delicious and thoroughly drinkable. Okay, so it is quiet – but when you want it to be, this wine is a highly civilised companion.

Lontue Sauvignon Blanc 1996 14.5 C

Delicious, calm, classy, fresh, hints of ripe fruit, balanced, exceedingly drinkable.

ENGLISH WINE — WHITE

Leeford's Vineyard English Wine 1995 10 C

Expensive, unbalanced, awkwardly fruited and quite oddly conceived. I cannot think anything but sentiment puts this wine on M&S shelves.

FRENCH WINE — RED

Beaujolais Sapin 1996 12 C

Cherries – who'll buy my ripe cherries? (Few people, I would have thought, at a fiver a bunch.)

Bordeaux Matured in Oak, AC Bordeaux 1993 12 D

Bourgogne Rouge Tastevinage 1993 11 D

Some gamy inclination but little style as it limps its way home.

Cepage Counoise VdP d'Oc, Domaine Jeune 1996 15.5 C

This is, as likely as not, the only 100 per cent counoise grape variety wine on sale at a British supermarket. Counoise? Hardly famous, it pops up as 2 per cent of a few Chateauneuf-du-Papes. In this manifestation it is strikingly soft yet alive with ripe tannins and has a huge weight of brambly fruit in the mouth. A very intriguing wine of class, style and delicious eccentricity.

Chateau de Santenay, Mercurey 1994 10 E

So dull I'd rather drink pineapple juice.

Chateauneuf-du-Pape, Quiot 1995 13 E

It's good, but I'd rather drink counoise (qv) at half the price.

Classic Claret Chateau Cazeau 1995 13.5 C

Domaine de Belle Feuille Cotes du Rhone 1995 11 C

Domaine St Pierre VdP de l'Herault, Domaines Virginie 1996 13.5 B

Very ripe and raunchy. Youngsters will like it.

Fitou, Domaine de Tauch Oak Aged 1993 15 C

Although one can't escape the nagging suspicion that this wine is a polite, anglicised Fitou made specifically for the orderly palates of M&S customers, there is a lot of soft, deliciously drinkable fruit here. Warm, ineffably plumply textured and willing, this is an attractive glug of immediate charm.

Fleurie Sapin 1996 13.5 E

Very drinkable. Has sufficient character and style to make you forget it's a beaujolais. And then you see that eight quid price tag!

French Country Red VdP des Pyrenees-Orientales, Vignerons Catalans 1996 13 B

Full Red, Cotes du Roussillon Villages (1 litre) 13 C

Gold Label Cabernet Sauvignon VdP d'Oc, Domaines Virginie 1995 15 C

Soft and very delicious with sufficient depth of warm, plummy fruit and finely knitted tannin to make it a brilliant glugging wine and a bottle to go with roasts and casseroles.

Gold Label Pinot Noir, Domaines Virginie VdP d'Oc 1994 12 C

House Red Wine 13 B

Margaux 1993 12.5 E

Merlot Moueix 1993 13 D

Moueix St Emilion 1993 13 E

Pinot Noir VdP d'Oc 1994 13.5 C

This would, it strikes me, be a ten-quid bottle (or much more)

if it said Volnay on the label. But it doesn't. It says Vin de Pays d'Oc – hicksville to the uninformed.

Syrah 'Domaine de Mandeville' VdP d'Oc 1996 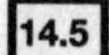 C

Syrah-like young beaujolais but much tastier and better with food. A real satisfying glug here.

FRENCH WINE WHITE

Chablis 1995 12.5 D

Chardonnay 'Domaine de Mandeville', VdP d'Oc 1996 14.5 C

Delicate fruit (hints of melon) with a lovely lemonic, nutty finish. Cannot take pungent food, but great with salad and grilled prawns, and fish cakes.

Cotes de Gascogne Vin de Pays, Plaimont 1996  

Very refreshing – in the glugging style of fruitiness.

French Country White Vin de Pays, Vignerons Catalans 1996  

Reasonable price but lacks bite on the finish.

Gold Label Chardonnay VdP d'Oc, Domaines Virginie 1996  C

Mild-mannered and can meet the in-laws without upsetting anyone.

House White Wine 12.5 B

Jeunes Vignes, La Chablisienne 1994 12 D

Montagny Premier Cru, Cave de Buxy 1994 15.5 D

Montagny as I remember it! Brilliantly textured, plump and edgily rich, with good vegetal undertones, thoroughly pleasant and balanced. Great with all sorts of fish and poultry dishes.

Petit Chablis 1996 13.5 D

Clean, mineral-edged, very fresh and lively.

Rose de Syrah VdP d'Oc, Domaines Virginie 1996 14 C

The cosmetic edge is saved from complete tartness by the crisp acidity. Excellent with back-garden fish barbecues.

Sancerre Les Ruettes 1995 12 D

Vin de Pays du Gers White, Plaimont 1996 14.5 B

Well-priced, well-fruited, well-adjusted all round. Nice pear/pineapple touch on the finish.

Viognier 'Domaine de Mandeville', VdP d'Oc 1996 15 C

Gentle apricot fruit, whistle-clean and fresh, with an excellent balanced finish of subtle peach and a vague hint of lime.

Vouvray Domaine de la Pouvraie 1996 15 C

Medium-bodied, slightly off-dry. But a brilliant aperitif. The fruit has a wet-wool edge to it and the acidity also saves the wine from sweetness. It will improve in bottle, if laid down, for several years. Delicious prospect for AD 2000 and beyond.

White Burgundy, Caves de Lugny 1995 11 C

GERMAN WINE — WHITE

Hock, Tafelwein 1996 (1 litre) 11 C

Somewhat dull.

Liebfraumilch, Klosterhof 1996

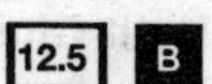

If you must drink Lieb, this is as good as any – and decently priced. A glass, well chilled, as a summer aperitif would be a not unattractive prospect on a hot evening.

ISRAELI WINE — WHITE

Galilee Golan Chardonnay 1994

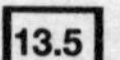

D

Expensive curiosity. Has texture and flavour but is too expensive and finishes with its style cramped. But a most respectable stab at chardonnay from an unlikely source. If it was £3.99 it would be a winner.

ITALIAN WINE — RED

Canfera Single Vineyard VdT di Toscana 1994 13 E

Interesting texture but the cherry-ripe fruit is adolescent and the finish mawkish. It would be a good wine at £3.99.

Chianti Roberta Sorelli 1995 13.5 C

Almost cherry-sweet on the finish. A mild red which would be better chilled – and drunk with barbecued meats and fish.

Italian Red Table Wine (1 litre) 14 C

Merlot del Veneto, Casa Girelli NV 12 B

Villa Cafaggio Chianti Classico 1995 13 D

Has an uncharacteristic sweetness on the finish. Spoils the attempt to build a classy wine.

ITALIAN WINE WHITE

Bianco di Puglia 1996 13.5 B

Clean, fresh, very respectable – not a lot of excitement but young and well served with good clean fruit. Good with fish and chips.

Chardonnay delle Tre Venezie 12 C

Frascati Superiore DOC (Estate Bottled) 1996 13 C

Good flavour – but a mite expensive.

Italian White Table Wine (1 litre) 13.5 C

Orvieto Classico 1996 14 C

Crisp and nutty – almost elegant. Good with spaghetti alla vongole.

Pinot Grigio delle Tre Venezie 13.5 C

MEXICAN WINE RED

Parras Valley Cabernet Sauvignon/Merlot 1994 14 C

Interesting vegetal aroma leads to some delicious fruit which is truly impressive. Very highly polished wine of dry, wry classiness.

NEW ZEALAND WINE RED

Kaituna Hills Cabernet/Merlot, Marlborough 1995 13.5 C

Certainly arouses the palate and the nose. But whether it's a sympathetic arousal I'm not convinced. The vegetality is what gets at you. And the ragged edge to the texture.

Saints Hawkes Bay Cabernet Merlot 1994 13.5 

NEW ZEALAND WINE WHITE

Kaituna Hills Gisborne Chardonnay 1996  

Rich, well-textured (melon spread thickly on velvet), well-balanced, well-priced, attractive all round.

Kaituna Hills Gisborne Chardonnay Semillon 1996 14.5 C

Great shellfish wine. Warm, soft fruit on the tongue which arrives through an aromatic entrance suggesting something leaner, meaner and more mineral-intensive. Still, it's very tasty, attractively balanced.

Kaituna Hills Marlborough Sauvignon Blanc 1996 15 D

Lovely grassy edge to firm, well-defined fruit of flavour and class.

Saints Gisborne Chardonnay 1995 14 D

SOUTH AFRICAN WINE RED

Cabernet Sauvignon Coastal Region KWV 1993 13.5 C

You won't believe cabernet can be made this puppyish and all-over-your-tongue friendly.

Shiraz Coastal Region KWV 1993 14.5 C

Shiraz wearing its jazzy outdoor clothes: soft, colourful, bursting with personality.

Stellenbosch Merlot 1996 14.5 C

Tasty, nicely leathery, dry but soft and ripe, and a lovely savoury edge to the fruit.

SOUTH AFRICAN WINE WHITE

Madeba Dry White 1996 12 C

Rather blowsy and ripe. Needs a rich fish dish on the side.

Madeba Reserve Chardonnay/Sauvignon Blanc 1996 13.5 C

Rather rich. Food necessary here.

McGregor Chardonnay 1996 13.5 C

Pleasant if not hugely gripping for the money.

McGregor Chenin Blanc 1996 13.5 C

Perderburg Cellar Sauvignon Blanc 1996 13 C

Hints of grass upfront but not much of a lawn out back – it finishes weakly.

SPANISH WINE RED

Bodegas Age Tempranillo Rioja 1994 14.5 C

Rioja fans' dream of a red: vanilla-textured, rapaciously fruity in the throat and accommodating with chorizo and chicken stew.

Gran Calesa Costers del Segre 1992 17 D

Savoury, rich, vibrant, dry yet softly voluptuous and fruity on the finish, this is lovely textured wine of great charm and flavoured, aromatic warmth.

Marques de Romeral Gran Reserva Rioja 1988 10 D

Flabby and knock-kneed, it seems pitiful to pit it against food let alone fork out seven quid for it.

Penascal Vino de Mesa Tinto, Castilla y Leon NV 13.5 C

Rioja Bodegas AGE 13 C

Roseral Rioja Crianza 1993 13 C

SPANISH WINE — WHITE

Moscatel de Valencia 14 C

URUGUAYAN WINE — RED

Uruguayan Merlot 1996 16 C

Real bite! Lots of flavour, depth, fruit, tannin, vigour, acidity and a brilliant texture to call it all off. Terrific food wine as well as a great barbecue glugger!

Uruguayan Tannat 1996 14.5 C

Warm, rustic, slightly woody aroma leads to full rich fruit with a very dry finish. The centre of the fruit is ripe plum as if oven-warm. Individual flavour all round.

URUGUAYAN WINE — WHITE

Uruguayan Chardonnay 1996 13.5 C

Fresh with a nutty finish. Very attractive. Touch pricey for the style, though.

Uruguayan Sauvignon/Gewurztraminer 1996 13.5 C

Interesting, even though the sauvignon well dominates the gewurz, and there is a hint of spice to fresh fruit.

USA WINE — RED

Canyon Road Cabernet Sauvignon 1994 16 D

A most coolly classy wine. Has a superb balance of fruit, acid and wood. These three strike energetically and authentically in harmony.

USA WINE — WHITE

Canyon Road Chardonnay 1995 14 D

FORTIFIED WINE

Cream Sherry 14 C

Fino Sherry 16 C

Delicate yet slyly fruity. A fino to bring wine lovers back to sherry?

Medium Amontillado Sherry 13 C

Rich Cream Sherry 15.5 C

SPARKLING WINE/CHAMPAGNE

Asti Spumante Consorzio 13 D

Bluff Hill Sparkling Wine (New Zealand) 13.5 D

Cava (Spain) 14 C

Champagne Chevalier de Melline, Premier Cru Blanc de Blancs 12 G

Champagne Orpale 1985 10 H

Oudinot Brut Champagne 16 F

This is one of the softest, most deliciously fruity champagnes at any supermarket anywhere. It has a delicate citric finish to complete its charms.

Oudinot Rose Champagne 14 F

Delightful rose – it justifies its soppy colour and steep price by being aromatically enticing, fruity in a most gentle way, with a finish of finesse.

Rosato Spumante (Italy) 12 C

Seppelt Chardonnay Blanc de Blanc Bottle Fermented Brut 1994 (Australia) 15 E

Delicate and delicious. As good as bubbly gets at this price.

Veuve de la Lalande Brut 10 C

Veuve de la Lalande Rose 12 C

Veuve de Medts, Premier Cru Brut (France) 14.5 G

Vintage Champagne, St Gall, Premier Cru Brut 1990 13 G

Vintage Oudinot Grand Cru 1989 13.5 G

Yarden Blanc de Blancs Bottle Fermented Brut NV (Israel) 13.5 E

Very elegant. As good as a Cava – but, alas, at twice the price.

Marks & Spencer
Michael House
57 Baker Street
London W1A 1DN
Tel 0171 935 4422
Fax 0171 487 2679

Summerplonk 1997

MORRISONS

ARGENTINIAN WINE RED

Balbi Vineyard Mendoza Rouge 1995 15.5 B

AUSTRALIAN WINE RED

Coldridge Shiraz/Cabernet Sauvignon 1996 

The Aussie version of peasant plonk. Thus, it lacks the backbone of Spanish, Italian and southern French peasants who do not bend over backwards to please – as does this soft, somewhat soppily fruity wine. Anyway, Australian peasants all drink beer.

Lindemans Bin 45 Cabernet Sauvignon 1995 13 D

I suppose one can imagine enjoying a glass, but it is trying to be liked so unimaginatively, it's embarrassing. I prefer more character in wine, as in people – especially at this price.

Lindemans Bin 50 Shiraz 1994 

Expensive for the style, which is puppyishly fruit.

Penfolds Bin 35 Shiraz Cabernet 1994 

Penfolds Rawsons Retreat Bin 35 1995  

Respectable rather than raunchy.

AUSTRALIAN WINE — WHITE

Coldridge Chenin Blanc/Chardonnay 1996 

C

Very prettily perfumed fruit with a cosmetic edge. Pleasant enough tipple in warm weather.

Lindemans Bin 65 Chardonnay 1996 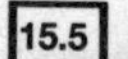

B

Delicious combination of butter, hazelnuts and melon undercut by a perfectly weighted uptide of acidity.

Penfolds Rawsons Retreat Bin 21 Semillon/Chardonnay/Colombard 1996 

C

Loaded with flavour and rich layers of fruit, it is nevertheless difficult to justify paying more for a summer wine.

Wyndham Estate TR2 Medium Dry White Wine 1995 

Sweet and sour-faced wine of oddly disconcerting charms.

BRAZILIAN WINE — RED

Amazon Cabernet Sauvignon 13.5 

BRAZILIAN WINE — WHITE

Amazon Chardonnay 

C

BULGARIAN WINE RED

Bear Ridge Gamza NV 12 B

CHILEAN WINE RED

Entre Rios Chilean Red 15.5 B

Stowells of Chelsea Chilean Merlot Cabernet (3-litre box) 10 G

CHILEAN WINE WHITE

Castillo de Molina Chardonnay 1995 14 C

Rich but not over-rich, nutty but not barking, elegant but a touch pushy. Great with rich fish and poultry dishes.

Castillo de Molina Chardonnay Reserva 1996 16 C

Very elegantly attired, rich and characterful, this is a splendid example of how mature in feel a young Chilean chardonnay can surprisingly be. It hums with flavour and it is irresistibly drinkable.

Castillo de Molina Sauvignon Blanc 1996 13 C

Entre Rios Chilean White 15 B

Gato Blanco Sauvignon Blanc, Lontue Valley 1996 16 B

Brilliant, crisp, textured fruit of length, style, elegance and subtlety which is perfect for hot-weather lip-wetting. It is excellent with fish, excellent value, excellent all round. It is high-quality sipping (if you must consume your white wine this way).

Stowells of Chelsea Chilean Sauvignon Blanc (3-litre box)

ENGLISH WINE WHITE

Three Choirs Estates Premium 1993

FRENCH WINE RED

Bourgogne 1994 10 D

It is true that expensive, rough burgundy like this goes surprisingly well with a roast hen, but you still have to part with seven quid for the wine and then there's the small matter of the hen. Seven quid is better spent elsewhere at Morrisons than here.

Cellier la Chouf, Minervois

Chateau de Flaugergues Coteaux du Languedoc 1995 14 D

Dry, rich, very dry and full of herb-packed brambly fruit. Lovely elegant food wine.

Chateau de Lauree Bordeaux Rouge 1995 14.5 B

Chateauneuf-du-Pape Domaine du Vieux Lazaret 1994 13.5 E

Very savoury and suave wine with a compacted, burnt edge to its finish. It has the smooth, elegant style of a good Chateauneuf with the warm herbal overtones softly controlled.

Corbieres Les Fenouillets 1995 15 B

£2.95! Doesn't seem credible. What do you do, Stuart, smuggle bottles out under your jumper? Why put up with the ferry port fracas when there's this number lying fruity and dry on Morrisons' shelves?

Coteaux du Languedoc NV 15.5 B

Amazingly well-turned out for the money: rich, softly textured and ripe, dry (good tannins), balanced and has some real hints of class. The alert palate might even detect, yawn yawn, the hint of chocolate in it. A chump chop will soon see off subtleties like this, leaving you mere tasty fruit.

Cotes du Rhone Villages 1995 14 C

Cotes du Ventoux 1995 14 B

Good lip-smackin', throat-throbbin' savoury finish to some decently rustic fruit. Brilliant value for barbecues.

Cotes du Luberon 1995 14.5 B

One of Morrisons' best barbecue reds: a characterfully dry wine of substance and acute drinkability. Complex? No. Rich? Not especially. True to itself? Absolutely.

Cotes du Rhone (half bottle) 13.5 A

Usefully fruity wine in a bottle sized to suit the modest tippler. A dry, approachable wine of simple charms. Also available in 75cl-1.5 litre sizes.

Cotes du Roussillon, Morrisons  B

Ridiculously down-to-earth in everything including, felicitously, price. It is dry, soft, gently rounded at the edges and has some degree of character. It is perfectly brilliant value for summer barbecue parties.

Domaine du Crouzel Corbieres 1995 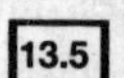 

The soft, lovely-to-meet-you level of southern French red. More raunch please! (Goes best with lunch, raunch.)

La Source Cabernet Sauvignon VdP d'Oc 1994 14 B

La Source Merlot VdP d'Oc 1994 13.5 C

La Source Syrah VdP d'Oc 1995  B

Simple, tasty, eminently acquirable and drinkable, well fleshed out on the finish. A good food and glugging red.

Le Millenaire Cotes du Roussillon Villages 1994 13.5 

Margaux 1994 11 E

The label says it all, really. 'Margaux!' it shouts. That stands for bullshit, bumptiousness, blather and bad value.

Marquis de l'Estouval, VdP de l'Herault 1995 13 A

Montregnac Bergerac 1994 13 B

Regnie, Duboeuf 1994 12 D

Renaissance Buzet 1994 14 C

Stowells of Chelsea Claret Bordeaux Rouge (3-litre box) 13 G

Vin de Pays de l'Aude Red (half bottle) 13 A

Has hints of dry scrubland which give the appley fruit some suggestion of its provenance. Also available in 75cl-1.5 litre sizes.

Winter Hill VdP de l'Aude 1995 15 B

FRENCH WINE — WHITE

Cascade Sauvignon Bordeaux 1994 10 B

Chais Cuxac Chardonnay VdP d'Oc 1996 15.5 C

A superbly well-balanced chardonnay of style and class. It has real depth to its fruit, no blowsiness or textured coarseness, and it has great versatility with food: soups, salads, chicken and fish. It is staggeringly good value when compared with some of the Burgundian stuff.

Chateau de Lauree Bordeaux 1995 12.5 B

Chateau Saint Galier, Graves 1995 14 C

Classy, mineral-edged fruit here. Good choice for fish and barbecued prawns, etcetera.

Cotes du Luberon 1996 14.5 B

Fresh-faced, clean, youthful, crisply turned out and a little nutty – can you think of a more amusing companion to spend an afternoon in the garden with? Especially if sardines or somesuch oceanic debutante is sizzling on the fire?

Cotes du Roussillon 11 B

Has a flat finish which is not expressive of wit or style.

Entre Deux Mers 1995 12 B

Ginestet Graves Blanc 1994 13 C

J. P. Chenet, Cinsault Rose 1995 12 B

La Source Chardonnay VdP de l'Aude 1996 14 B

Languedoc's most engaging under-three-quid chardonnay. Has bite, balance and some hints of richness.

La Source Sauvignon Blanc VdP d'Oc 1996 15 B

Ah, the many virtues of this splendid little wine! Let me count the ways it thrills me: 1. The smell. 2. The fruit. 3. The price. 4. The plastic cork. A wine of plasticity, price and proper sauvignon fruit.

La Source Syrah Rose VdP d'Oc 1995 13 B

Le Millenaire Cotes du Roussillon 1994 

Macon-Villages Domaine Jean-Pierre Teissedre 1994 

At nigh on a fiver, it's asking a lot. However, it does have some blunt character to it of warm vegetality but as a specimen of delicious fruit, chardonnay at that, to compare it with similarly priced specimens of the same grape from Chile, South Africa, Languedoc and southern Italy is to find this wine lacking.

Meursault Pierre Matrot 1990 

Montregnac Sauvignon, Bergerac 1995 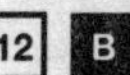

This is reasonable enough, for a French sauvignon at £3.30, but compare it with Gato Blanco at the same price, same grape, and you see the gulf which separates the ordinary from the truly classy.

Muscadet Sevre et Maine, Morrisons  

Has something in its fruit and acidity which rings a bell (i.e. reminds the ancient tippler of the excellence of muscadet when Napoleon was the French Republic's head barman) but it's only an echo.

Pouilly Fume Pierre Guery 1995 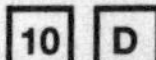 

Insipid and uninspired. Morrisons only stock it because there are still clots in the wood who see the words 'Pouilly Fume' on the label and think 'Wow!' Let us pity these poor creatures.

Rose d'Anjou, Morrisons  

The label speaks true! It *is* fruity and elegant as claimed and it is perfect, well chilled, as a summer slurp. I would add it's cheap – for a decent rose – and it has a beautiful plastic cork.

Terret Vin de Pays Lurton 1994 12 B

Tradition Gewurztraminer Vin d'Alsace, Preiss-Zimmer 1995 14 D

Expensive but worth the entrance money for the quirkily exotic edge of smoky spiciness to the fruit. Brilliant with oriental food.

Vin de Pays de l'Aude White (half bottle) 13.5 A

It's simplicity itself but has some crisp charm and a level of fruit to tickle anyone's palate on a warm day. Also available in 75cl-1.5 litre sizes.

Vouvray Jean Michel 1995 10 C

Winter Hill White 1995 13.5 B

GERMAN WINE WHITE

Flonheimer Adelberg Kabinett Johannes Egberts 1995 13 B

Franz Reh Auslese 1994 12 C

Franz Reh Kabinett 1994 11 B

Franz Reh Spatlese 1993 12 B

Seafish Dry Rheinhessen 1995 12 B

Tries so hard to be liked! It is, however, somewhat of a dull dog – even at £3.09.

Stowells of Chelsea Liebfraumilch (3-litre box) 12 F

Zimmermann Riesling NV 13.5 C

More zip than its rivaner cousin, it has the citricity of riesling with some of its subtle richness – but in a dry form. It's just so ridiculously uncompetitively priced at £3.99!

Zimmermann Rivaner NV

Not a bad stab at grape crushing. A glass, chilled, after a day at the coal face would be acceptable enough – you could employ the remainder as a foot bath (but I'm being very cruel to a decent wine here – besides, your feet would have to be abnormally tiny).

GREEK WINE RED

Mavrodaphne of Patras 11 C

GREEK WINE WHITE

Kourtaki Vin de Crete 1995

Crete was the place I once tasted the worst wine in the world: a heavily oxidised red retsina of such inflammability it could have usefully gone into a paraffin lamp. This white, dry example of Cretan oenology is not so vile.

ITALIAN WINE RED

Chianti Classico Uggiano 1995

A soupy, jammy chianti of a curious style. It's probably at its best with pastas with rich meaty sauces.

Chianti dei Colli Fiorentini Uggiano 1994

Has greater acidity and bite than other Uggiano chiantis. Perhaps its particular provenance is the reason and this gives it a lighter, zippier feel in the mouth, with muted earthiness. An attractive glug and versatile food wine (chicken, roasts, pastas).

Chianti Riserva Uggiano 1991

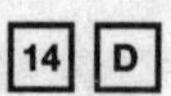

The most expensive Uggiano offering and rightly so: it's an impressive, correctly Tuscan red of rich dry flavours which summon up hints of the most hearty aspects of the landscape and cuisine of its native region. It would be excellent with lamb roasted with rosemary. It also goes brilliantly with dishes using Parmesan cheese.

Chianti Uggiano 1995

Better than its Classico big brother (and over a quid less). Has typical Tuscan earthy overtones to a decent level of rich plummy fruit.

Eclisse VdT di Puglia Rosso

Merlot del Veneto, Vigneti del Sole 1996 13.5 B

Cheap, cheerful, lightly fruity company. Probably best chilled with a fish stew.

Montepulciano d'Abruzzo Vigneti del Sole 1995 13.5 B

Valpolicella (half bottle) 12 A

Has some warmth. But so does a three-bar electric fire. Also available in 75cl-1.5 litre sizes.

ITALIAN WINE — WHITE

Eclisse VdT di Puglia Bianco 12 B

Frascati Superiore 1996 12.5 A

Has a gentle energy and bite to its meagre fruit. Also available in 75cl-1.5 litre sizes.

Orvieto Classico Uggiano 1995 13.5 B

A clean, fresh wine of decency and good citizenship, but it might just exhibit a bit more character.

Soave (half bottle) 12 A

Not especially suave (or smooth or polite), but then that's misnomers all over . . . Also available in 75cl-1.5 litre sizes.

Stowells of Chelsea Chardonnay (3-litre box) 13.5 G

MOROCCAN WINE RED

Cabernet Syrah 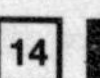

Not as rampantly rich and savoury as it has been, but it's still soft and highly drinkable – and well able to cope with a range of meaty dishes. It's a jammy wine of warmth and subtle richness.

PORTUGUESE WINE RED

Bairrada Reserva, Borges 1994 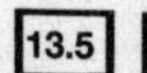 

There's a hiccup to the fruit as it finishes in the throat when you'd prefer to supply your own satisfied hiccups. This might disappear with food, but it mars an otherwise reasonable show.

Soveral Tinto de Mesa 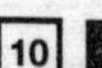 

Val Longa Country Wine NV  

PORTUGUESE WINE WHITE

Val Longa Country Wine NV  

ROMANIAN WINE RED

Classic Pinot Noir 1994 13.5 B

Not as gamy or gripping as previous vintages. Bit uncertain of itself and light on the finish.

ROMANIAN WINE WHITE

Romanian Late Harvest Chardonnay 1985 14 B

SOUTH AFRICAN WINE RED

Bottelary Winery Pinotage, Stellenbosch 1995 13.5 C

Bovlei Winery Merlot 1995 15.5 B

Cracker for the money: warm, rich, aromatic, reasonably deep and gently leathery (leather with some degree of polish to it) and very well balanced. It is excellent company for roasts, cheeses and vegetables, pastas, risotti and sausages.

South African Red, Morrisons  B

Thoroughly warm and friendly and unspeakably drinkable – if you don't mind the mollycoddling it gives the throat on the way down. It has a kind of linctus effect.

SOUTH AFRICAN WINE WHITE

Bovlei Winery Sauvignon Blanc 1996

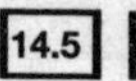

Deliciously nutty and fresh – great accompaniment to all fish dishes.

Cape Country Chardonnay 1996

Somewhat muddy fruit of uncertain direction.

Faircape Chenin Blanc 1996

Good summer tippling here. Trips neatly over the tongue with gentle lemonic steps, crisp and positive, and its style is very suited to all fish dishes. There is a faint floral quality to it which, whilst never intrusive, gives it a seasonal deliciousness.

Faircape Sauvignon Blanc 1995

South African White Wine

Doesn't quite come up to scratch on the finish, though it has reasonable attractive fruit lightly fleshed out in the modern manner.

Stowells of Chelsea Chenin Blanc (3-litre box)

SPANISH WINE RED

Good Spanish Red

At £2.59 (at time of writing – hand steady as a rock after grasping its seventieth glass of the day), this wine is no pain to acquire and no pain to drink. True, its price tag generates more excitement than its fruit, but let us not gainsay the fruity softness of the wine which is commendably soupy.

Navajas Rioja 1995 15 C

Remonte Navarra Crianza Cabernet Sauvignon 1992 15.5 C

Rioja Navajas Reserva 1990 14 D

Minty, stylish and decently fruity – but at six quid it requires more. And it provides more (albeit a touch of it): texture and fair fruit.

Stowells of Chelsea Tempranillo (3-litre box) 14 F

Torres Sangredetoro 1994 16 C

Best vintage of this old warhorse for some while. Has gently spicy, warmly textured fruit, ripe and rich but deliciously coated with a dry tannic shellac. Great with casseroles, etc.

SPANISH WINE WHITE

Solana Torrontes Treixadura 1994 15 C

You might think twice before spending the touch over four quid needed to acquire this eccentricity, but if you want something different, exotic, summery and delicious, then hesitate not. Local peasant grape vinified into something crisp and flavourful for barbecued, grilled, poached and even raw fish.

USA WINE — RED

Blossom Hill, California 10 C

Californian Red NV 14 B

A dry but cheerfully fruity wine with hints of gunsmoke, railway sleepers and one-horse saloons.

Sutter Home Cabernet Sauvignon 1993 13.5 C

Willamette Oregon Pinot Noir 1993 13.5 E

USA WINE — WHITE

Blossom Hill, California 10 C

Californian White NV 12.5 B

Glen Ellen Proprietor's Reserve Chardonnay 1995 16 C

Developing more vegetality as it ages but still a richly textured, plump chardonnay of flavour, depth and real engaging fruitiness. It offers a lovely glass of wine to all the senses.

Sebastiani White Zinfandel 1995 10 C

Sutter Home California Chardonnay 1995 13.5 C

Creamy, very attractively flavoured fruit of some elegance and charm. It just doesn't convince me of its integrity.

Willamette Valley Chardonnay, Oregon 1993 14.5 E

A lot of money but a lot of fruit: mature, rich, rampantly deep and gummy (and yummy), it is a ripe, full wine of savouriness, texture and old-style (in the best sense of the word) burgundian rusticality yet finesse.

FORTIFIED WINE

Rozes Ruby 13 C

Rozes Special Reserve 11 D

Rozes Tawny 12.5 C

SPARKLING WINE/CHAMPAGNE

Asti Spumante Gianni (Italian) 11 C

Paul Herard Blanc de Noirs Brut Champagne (half bottle) 14 D

Paul Herard Blanc de Noirs Demi Sec Champagne (half bottle) 12 D

Raimat Sparkling Chardonnay (Spain)	15	D
Seaview Brut	14	D
Seppelt Great Western Brut	15	C

Wm Morrison Supermarkets
Wakefield 41 Industrial Estate
Wakefield
W Yorks WFl 0XF
Tel 01924 870000
Fax 01924 821250

Summerplonk 1997

SAFEWAY

ARGENTINIAN WINE RED

Alamos Ridge Cabernet Sauvignon, Mendoza 1994

Dry Bordeaux style without the austerity. Selected stores.

Balbi Vineyard Malbec 1996

Mendoza Red 1996, Safeway

Terrific value for money here. A dry yet rollingly rich-edged wine which reserves its best speech for the final curtain.

ARGENTINIAN WINE WHITE

Alamos Ridge Chardonnay, Mendoza 1996

Complex, individual, hints of controlled richness, great balance, firm acidity. An excellent chardonnay of style and character. Selected stores.

Balbi Syrah Rose 1996

Needs to be well chilled for its richness to shine through. It's certainly a good food wine, fish or meat, but for me it's a mite too cloyingly fruity as a general glugging wine.

AUSTRALIAN WINE RED

Breakaway Grenache/Shiraz, McLaren 1995 14 C

There might be the odd bottle of the '95 left, but the '96 should be coming in by the time this book appears (not available for tasting at time of going to press).

Farms Cabernet/Merlot, Barossa Valley 1992 10 F

Spineless and far too pricey. Top fifty stores.

Hardys Bankside Shiraz 1995 14 D

Soft and agreeable – lacks punch on the finish, though.

Hardys Collection Coonawarra Cabernet Sauvignon 1994 14 E

Hardys Stamp Grenache/Syrah 1996 13 C

Jacob's Creek Dry Red 1993 15 C

Lindemans Pyrus, Coonawarra 1993 14 F

Very expensive but worthy – if not magnificent. The texture and fruit are high class but it is a touch contrived in style. Top fifty stores.

Mount Hurtle Shiraz 1994 14 E

Penfolds Bin 407 Cabernet Sauvignon 1993 15 E

Deeply classy fruit and tannic scaffolding give the whole construct richness, ornamentation and solidity.

Penfolds Clare Valley Shiraz/Cabernet Sauvignon 1994 15.5 D

By the time this book comes out the '95 should be coming into stores (not tasted at time of going to press) but I'm told the '94 should still be available here and there.

Penfolds Koonunga Hill Shiraz Cabernet 1992 14 C

Penfolds Rawsons Retreat Bin 35 1995 13.5 C

Usual decent turnout.

Peter Lehmann Barossa Cabernet Sauvignon 1995 15.5 E

An expensive but very interesting, tannically well-shaped cabernet. Selected stores.

Rosemount Estate Cabernet Sauvignon 1995 14 D

Stylish and drinkable but a touch expensive. Should be coming into selected stores as this book comes out.

Rosemount Shiraz/Cabernet 1995 15 C

South Eastern Australia Oaked Cabernet Sauvignon 1995, Safeway 15 C

South Eastern Australia Oaked Shiraz 1996 14 C

South Eastern Australia Shiraz/Ruby Cabernet 1996, Safeway 15 C

Stoneyfell Metala Shiraz/Cabernet Sauvignon, Langhorne Creek 1994 13.5 D

Dazzlingly labelled like a tonic sherry of pre-rationing days. Very ripe and squashy. Top fifty stores.

Wolf Blass Yellow Label Cabernet Sauvignon 1993 13.5 D

AUSTRALIAN WINE WHITE

Australian Chardonnay/Colombard 1996, Safeway 15.5 C

Lovely rich texture twitches over the tongue, flavoursome and frisky, young yet mature, and the result is classy and terrific value.

Australian Marsanne 1996, Safeway 12 D

Dull for the money – respectable but dull.

Australian Oaked Colombard 1996 13 C

Breakaway Grenache Rose 1996 11 C

Breakaway Sauvignon Blanc/Semillon 1996 13 C

Geoff Merrill Chardonnay 1994 13.5 E

Hardys Nottage Hill Chardonnay 1996 16 C

Superb soft, rolling texture. Brilliant fruit. Great balance.

Jacob's Creek Semillon/Chardonnay 1996

Jacob's Creek Riesling 1995

Penfolds Organic Chardonnay/Sauvignon Blanc, Clare Valley 1996

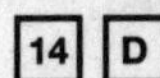

One of the classiest organic whites around: thick fruit of richness and flavour.

Penfolds Rawsons Retreat Bin 21 Semillon/Chardonnay/Colombard 1996

Richly textured, warmly fruity (some complexity on the finish where the acidity is most pertinent), this is an excellent vintage for this wine.

Peter Lehmann Chardonnay/Semillon, Barossa 1995

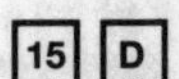

Rosemount Estate Chardonnay, Hunter Valley 1996

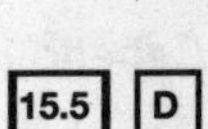

Elegance personified. A treat. Selected stores.

Rosemount Estate Semillon/Chardonnay 1995

Rosemount Estate Show Reserve Chardonnay 1995

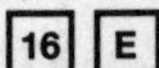

Gripping texture, soft as buttered muslin. Selected stores.

BULGARIAN WINE RED

Gorchivka Estate Selection Cabernet Sauvignon 1993 14 

BULGARIAN WINE WHITE

Chardonnay Reserva 1993 15 C

CHILEAN WINE RED

Caballo Loco No 1 13.5 

Decent enough but not a tenner's worth. Top fifty stores.

Caliterra Cabernet Sauvignon 1995 16.5 C

What flavour! What softness! What lingering depth of fruit! Chile, I kiss your feet.

Casa Lapostolle Cuvee Alexandre Merlot 1995 17 E

One of Chile's finest merlots. It's magnificently well endowed with deftly interwoven fruit and tannin. Masterly. Top fifty stores.

Chilean Cabernet Sauvignon, Lontue 1995, Safeway 17.5 C

Worth hunting down the last bottles although the '96 will be coming into stores as this book appears (not tasted at time of going to press).

Chilean Carignan, Maule Valley 1996, Safeway 14.5 C

Unusually earthy Chilean red. Has bite, style, character and subtle richness. Should just be coming into selected stores when this book comes out.

Palmeras Estate Oak Aged Cabernet Sauvignon, Nancagua 1995 15.5 C

What energy and brightness here! Has textured tannins, richness and depth. Great food wine.

Valdivieso Cabernet Franc 1995 15.5 

Lovely perfume, great depth, soft, rich, warmly textured fruit. A treat. Top fifty stores.

CHILEAN WINE WHITE

Caliterra Chardonnay 1996 15 C

Castillo de Molina Sauvignon Blanc 1996 13 C

Chilean Chardonnay 1996, Safeway 15.5 C

Chilean Dry White 1996, Safeway 13.5 B

Chilean Sauvignon Blanc, Lontue 1996, Safeway 13.5 C

Cordillera Estate Oak Aged Chardonnay, Casablanca 1996 13.5 C

One of the few Chilean chardonnays not to really excite me.

ENGLISH WINE — WHITE

Stanlake, Thames Valley Vineyards 1996, Safeway 13.5 C

Excellent looker (label-wise) but thin on fruit and crashes on the finish.

FRENCH WINE — RED

Beaujolais 1995, Safeway 12 C

Beaune Premier Cru Les Epenottes 1994 11 F

Top fifty stores.

Bourgueil 'Cuvee:Les Chevaliers' 1995 12 C

Vegetal, expensive. Selected stores.

Cabernet Sauvignon VdP d'Oc 1995, Safeway 15.5 C

Chateau des Gemeaux, Pauillac 1992 12.5 D

Chateau du Ragon, Bordeaux 1996 13 C

Very dry. Good with roast meats.

Chateau la Tour de Beraud, Costieres de Nimes 1994 14 C

There might be the odd bottle left, but the '95 should be coming in just as this book is published (not tasted at time of going to press).

Claret, Safeway 12 B

Cotes du Rhone 1995, Safeway 13 B

By the time this book appears, the '96 will possibly be coming into stores, but was not available for tasting at the time of going to press.

Cotes du Rhone Oak Aged 1995 14 C

Domaine du Bois des Dames Cotes du Rhone Villages 1995 14.5 C

Domaine Roche Vue Minervois 1995 15.5 C

Has colour, aroma, rich fruit, dryness, balance, tannin – it all adds up to a treat for eye and throat and with barbecued meats a great treat.

Domaine Vieux Manoir de Maransan, Cotes du Rhone 1995 13 C

Polished, very polished.

French Organic Vin de Table, Safeway 13 B

Gevrey-Chambertin Domaine Rossignol-Trapet 1993 11 F

Selected stores.

Hautes Cotes de Nuits Cuvee Speciale 1995 12 D

Selected stores.

La Cuvee Mythique Vin de Pays d'Oc 1994 15 D

Very classy blend of grapes. A dry, rich, herby, characterful wine of style. Selected stores.

Margaux 1993, Safeway 12 E

Nuits St George 1993, Safeway 10 E

Should still be available, but the '95 (not tasted as at going to press) will be coming in any minute now.

Oak Aged Medoc 1993 13 C

Oak-aged Claret NV, Safeway 13.5 C

Richemont Montbrun Old Vine Carignan VdP de l'Aude 1995 13 D

I loved it until the finish – too sentimental. Top fifty stores.

St-Julien 1994 (half bottle) 11 E

Volnay Domaine Michel Lafarge 1992 10 F

FRENCH WINE WHITE

Chablis Cuvee Domaine Yvon Pautre 1995, Safeway 10 D

Chardonnay VdP d'Oc 1995, Safeway 13 C

The '95 should still be available, I'm told, but the '96 will be coming into store any minute now – not tasted at the time of going to press.

Chateau du Plantier Entre Deux Mers 1996 14 C

Delightful tippling here – a wine of fresh, spring-flower fruit.

Cotes du Luberon Rose 1996, Safeway 13.5 B

Domaine de l'Ecu Muscadet de Sevre et Maine Sur Lie 1996 (Organic) 13 D

Expensive. Selected stores.

Domaine de Rivoyre Chardonnay VdP d'Oc 1995 15.5 C

Brilliance of texture, richness of fruit, poise and real class make this a bargain.

Domaine du Rey Vegetarian White Wine, VdP des Cotes de Gascogne 1996 13 C

Crisp and clean – what else can one say of it? Selected stores.

Domaine Latour-Giraud Meursault 1994 11 F

Domaine Vieux Manoir de Maransan, Cotes du Rhone 1996 14 C

A modern version of the earthy Rhone-style white – it's fruity, bustling, polished, and crisp to finish. Selected stores.

Hugh Ryman Chardonnay VdP d'Oc 1995 16 C

Subtle, balanced, incisive, very classy, calm, impressive. Rich food will disturb it but grilled white fish is perfect.

Premieres Cotes de Bordeaux, Safeway 11 C

Sancerre 'Les Bonnes Bouches' Domaine Henri Bourgeois 1996 11 E

A lot of money, nine quid. I expect a lot of wine for it.

Sauvignon de Touraine 1996, Safeway 13 C

It's white, yes, it's definitely white – and it's drinkable. Is it, though, a four-quid white? Selected stores.

Vin de Pays de Vaucluse 1996, Safeway 13.5 B

Clean as a surgeon's razor.

GERMAN WINE WHITE

Auslese 1994, Pfalz, Safeway 13.5 C

Gewurztraminer Pfalz 1995, Safeway 10 C

Hugh Ryman Almond Grove Riesling Dry, Pfalz 1993

HUNGARIAN WINE — RED

Chapel Hill Barrique-Aged Cabernet Sauvignon 1994

Should still be available but the '96 will be coming into stores at any moment (not tasted at time of going to press).

Chapel Hill Cabernet Sauvignon 1995, Safeway

Interesting, dry, food-friendly – but expensive.

Spring Time Red, Nagyrede 1996

More like autumn in its old leafy taste.

HUNGARIAN WINE — WHITE

Chapel Hill Barrique-fermented Chardonnay, Balaton 1995

Hungarian Cabernet Sauvignon Rose 1996, Safeway

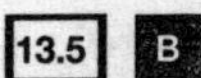

Not as fruity as it once was but still a reasonably polished specimen. Selected stores.

Hungarian Pinot Blanc, Nagyrede 1996, Safeway 14.5 B

Matra Mountain Pinot Grigio, Nagyrede 1996, Safeway 13.5 C

Very pleasant tipple – not exciting, perhaps, but very agreeable. Selected stores.

Matra Mountain Sauvignon Blanc, Nagyrede 1996, Safeway 13 C

Another fresh, clean Safeway bottle. Selected stores.

Neszmely Estate Barrique-Fermented Sauvignon Blanc 1995 15.5 C

Riverview Chardonnay/Pinot Gris, Neszmely 1996 13.5 C

Yet another respectable, crisp, dry white at Safeway.

ITALIAN WINE — RED

Amarone della Valpolicella Classico 1993 12 F

A lot of money. Too much. Top fifty stores.

Barolo Terre del Barolo 1992 12 E

Overpriced and underfruited. If it was £3.99 it would be fine. Hence its 12-point rating.

Casa di Giovanni 1994, Safeway

There may be the odd bottle left but the next vintage will be coming in as this book appears (not tasted at time of going to press).

Chianti 1995, Safeway

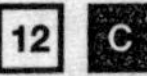

As for the Casa di Giovanni above.

Chianti Classico 1994, Safeway

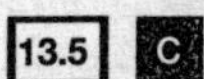

As for the chianti above.

Lambrusco Rosso, Safeway

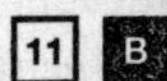

Montepulciano d'Abruzzo, Barrique Aged 1994

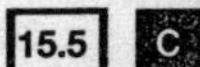

Tedeschi Capitel San Rocco Rosso 1991

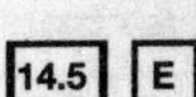

Tenuta San Vito Chianti 1995 (Organic)

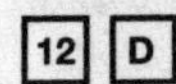

Very dry and inexpressive of not a lot more than the earth. Selected stores.

Young Vatted Teroldego, Atesino 1996, Safeway

A bold, softly fruity wine of plum and blackcurrant fruit. Good chilled with barbecues. Selected stores.

Zagara Nero d'Avola 1996 (Sicily)

Terrific texture (soft), good ripe fruit and deep flavour. Selected stores.

ITALIAN WINE — WHITE

Bianco del Lazio 1996, Safeway 13.5 B

Casa di Giovanni VdT di Sicilia 1996, Safeway 14 C

Intriguing bouquet, very attractive, and good fruit. An engaging wine with some claim to class.

Chardonnay delle Venezie 1996, Safeway 13.5 C

Rich, nutty Italian, not quite baroque but pleasantly ornamental on the tongue.

Lambrusco Rose, Safeway 10 B

Lambrusco, Safeway 10 B

Puglian White 1995, Safeway 14 C

Worth looking out for the odd bottle that may be left before the '95 comes into store (not tasted at time of going to press).

Sicilian Dry White 1996, Safeway 13.5 B

Light, dry picnic wine – good with sardines.

MOLDOVAN WINE — RED

Kirkwood Cabernet/Merlot 1995 15.5 B

MOLDOVAN WINE — WHITE

Kirkwood Chardonnay 1995

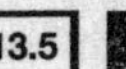

Getting to the end of its shelf-life, this fruit, but still great value.

MOROCCAN WINE — RED

Domaine Sapt Inour

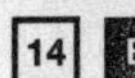

Warm, soft, soupy, excellent value for summer barbecues. Selected stores.

NEW ZEALAND WINE — WHITE

Millton Vineyard Barrel-fermented Chardonnay 1995

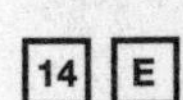

Montana Sauvignon Blanc 1996

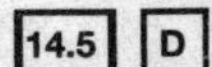

Good grassiness smoothly mown and well tended. Loss of impact on the finish but too individual and decently fruity to rate less.

Taurau Valley 1996

The Millton Vineyard Semillon/Chardonnay, Gisborne 1996 13 D

Clean and fresh, but a touch expensive for the overall simplicity of the style. Selected stores.

PORTUGUESE WINE RED

Fiuza Merlot, Ribatejo 1994 14 C

The odd bottle might still be left, but the '95 will be coming in any minute now – see below.

Fiuza Merlot, Ribatejo 1995 15 C

Lovely savoury fumes attached to this textured, dry, deep wine.

Tinto da Anfora, Alentejo 1992 12 D

Alas, not as exciting as once it was.

PORTUGUESE WINE WHITE

Bright Brothers Fernao Pires/Chardonnay, Ribatejo 1995 15.5 C

Vinho Regional Ribatejo, Falua 1996 13 B

SOUTH AFRICAN WINE RED

Cape Red 1996, Safeway 13.5 B

Jacana Cabernet Sauvignon/Merlot Reserve, Stellenbosch 1995 15 E

Heavy, serious, rich, tannic, dry, not a laugh in sight. Give it to a geriatric claret lover for Christmas. Selected stores.

Kleindal Pinotage 1996, Safeway 16.5 C

Brilliant lingering flavour and rounded softness of tone. Terrific balance makes this wine both deep and quaffable. Humming value for money.

Rosenview Cabernet Sauvignon, Stellenbosch 1996 14 C

Rosenview Cinsault 1996 14.5 C

Rosenview Merlot, Stellenbosch 1996 13 C

Villiera Estate Cabernet Sauvignon/Shiraz, Paarl 1995 15 D

Has a somewhat burnt edge to the fruit on the finish which lifts the finesse of the delivery. A lovely mellow wine of aplomb and stylish intent.

SOUTH AFRICAN WINE WHITE

Cape Dry White 1996, Safeway 14 B

Quagga Colombard/Chardonnay, Western Cape 1996, Safeway 13.5 B

South African Chenin Blanc, Swartland 1996, Safeway 13.5 B

Umfiki Sauvignon Blanc 1996 13 C

Vergelegen Chardonnay, Stellenbosch 1995 16 D

Warmth and depth of flavour, complexity, great charm and a lengthy presence on the palate.

Waterside White Colombard/Chardonnay 1996 14 C

SPANISH WINE RED

Cosme Palacio y Hermanos Rioja 1995 16 D

One of the tastiest riojas around: dry, rich, resoundingly well packed with fruit, and beautifully textured with assertive but not aggressive tannins. Selected stores.

Don Darias 14 B

Stowells of Chelsea Tempranillo (3-litre box) 14 F

Valdepenas Reserva 1991, Safeway 15 C

SPANISH WINE — WHITE

Wine	Rating	Price
Somontano Chardonnay 1995	15.5	C
Vina Malea Oaked Viura 1995	15.5	B

USA WINE — RED

Wine	Rating	Price
Fetzer Zinfandel 1993	14.5	D
Glen Ellen Merlot Proprietor's Reserve 1994	15	C

FORTIFIED WINE

Wine	Rating	Price
10 Year Old Tawny Port, Safeway	11	F
Cream Sherry, Safeway	13	C
Fino Sherry, Safeway	14	C
Lustau Old Amontillado Sherry (half bottle)	14	B
Lustau Old Dry Oloroso Sherry (half bottle)	14	B
Ruby Port, Safeway	12	D

Taylors LBV 1989 13.5 F

Vintage Character Port, Safeway 12.5 D

SPARKLING WINE/CHAMPAGNE

Albert Etienne Champagne Brut, Safeway 12 H

Rather raw on the finish. Top ninety-five stores.

Asti Spumante, Safeway 11 C

Chartogne-Taillet Champagne Brut Cuvee Sainte-Anne 12 G

Edwards & Chaffey Pinot Noir/Chardonnay 1992 (Australia) 15 E

The distant echo of marzipan on the rich fruit is quite lovely. A complex bubbly of greater interest and intrigue than many champagnes at twice the price.

Graham Beck Brut (South Africa) 13.5 E

J. Bourgeois Pere et Fils Champagne Brut 12.5 F

Lindauer Brut 13.5 D

Moscato Spumante, Safeway 12 C

Pol Acker Chardonnay Brut (France) 14 C

Saumur Brut, Safeway 14 D

Sparkling Chardonnay Brut, Safeway (Italy) 13.5 D

Veuve Clicquot Champagne Yellow Label Brut 12 H

Safeway plc
Safeway House
6 Millington Road
Hayes UB3 4AY
Tel 0181 848 8744
Fax 0181 573 1865

Summerplonk 1997

SAINSBURY'S

ARGENTINIAN WINE RED

Mendoza Cabernet Sauvignon/Malbec Peter Bright, Sainsbury's 15 B

Mendoza Country Red, Sainsbury's 15 B

Lovely level of rich fruit here plus an expensive texture. Great to slurp with or without food.

Mendoza Pinot Noir/Syrah, Sainsbury's 15 C

Mendoza Sangiovese, Sainsbury's 14.5 C

Juicy, fun, light to begin but rich to finish. Selected stores.

Mendoza Tempranillo, Sainsbury's 16 C

Watch out, rioja! This will give tempranillo fans everywhere something to slaver over – a rich, dark, exotic beauty of depth and very warm personality. Top seventy stores.

ARGENTINIAN WINE WHITE

Mendoza Country White, Sainsbury's 14 B

A curiously fruited wine for food (which it must have, it seems to me). The aroma is oddly cosmetic and talcum powdery and so is the fruit. But with a roast chicken these are assets.

Mendoza Torrontes, Sainsbury's 14 B

Bargain fish pie wine – or for a giant moules meuniere gathering. Top seventy stores.

Tupungato Chenin Chardonnay Peter Bright, Sainsbury's 14.5 C

AUSTRALIAN WINE RED

Bailey's Block 1920s Shiraz 1993 18 E

Will be 20 points in three years? One of Australia's great shirazes and therefore one of the most interesting syrah representatives in the whole wide world. It explodes with flavour, leathery, cassis-like but with a figgy undertone, and the finish is rich. It has superb tannins, fruit and acid. Top twenty-five stores.

Hardys Banrock Station Mataro/Grenache/ Shiraz 1996

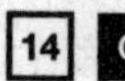

Restrained for an Aussie with a hint of vegetality to the fruit. It has a curious coy demeanour. Now – when did you last meet an Aussie like that?

Hardys Nottage Hill Cabernet Sauvignon/ Shiraz 1995

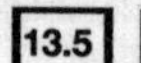

Hmm . . . okay, but a fiver?

Hardys Stamp Series Shiraz/Cabernet Sauvignon 1995

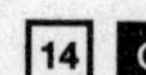

Jacob's Creek Shiraz Cabernet 1995

Respectable, respectable.

Lindemans Bin 45 Cabernet Sauvignon 1994 15 D

Seems more insistently rich than previous vintages. Quite deliciously cheeky. Offers excellent value under a fiver, this Aussie classic.

Lindemans Cawarra Shiraz/Cabernet Sauvignon 1996 14 C

Savoury, dry (but amply rich and fruity on the finish), gently relaxing and softly meaty. Selected stores.

Lindemans Padthaway Pinot Noir, Coonawarra 1995 13.5 E

Not bad as Aussie pinot goes – but I'm not sure this raspberry-scented vegetality and strawberry richness is worth eight quid. Top twenty-five stores.

Lindemans Pyrus Coonawarra 1992 15 F

The elegance and aplomb here is delightful to behold and experience. Lovely texture, minty fruit and a whiplash finish of soft, tannicky satin. A very fine wine indeed – but is it worth £12? Top twenty-five stores only.

Penfolds Bin 2 Shiraz/Mourvedre 1995 15.5 D

Rich, dry, stylish, this has fluidity of fruit yet tannic firmness of tone.

Penfolds Bin 389 Cabernet/Shiraz 1993 15 E

Rosemount Diamond Label Shiraz 1995 15 D

Such heavenly textured richness and flavour but delicate, mild meats and vegetable dishes will suit it, not robust ones. Top seventy stores.

Rosemount Estate Cabernet Sauvignon 1994 14 D

Rosemount Estate Shiraz/Cabernet 1995 15 C

Rothbury Estate South East Australian Cabernet Sauvignon 1993 13.5 D

St Hallett Cabernet Merlot 1994 13.5 E

Lots of money for such squidgy fruit. A great £3.50 tipple but not at nigh on eight quid. Selected stores.

Tarrawingee Shiraz Mourvedre, Sainsbury's 12 C

Tyrrells Cabernet Merlot, South Australia 1995 13 D

Expensive for the shortness of the excitement. Selected stores.

Wynns Cabernet Sauvignon, Coonawarra 1991 14.5 E

AUSTRALIAN WINE WHITE

Australian Chardonnay, Sainsbury's 14.5 C

A quiet, firm chardonnay which politely whispers. But this is a great improvement on the raucous shout of yesteryear's Aussie chardies!

Australian Semillon Sauvignon Blanc, Sainsbury's 15.5 C

Beautiful hand-in-hand wine. The semillon has bite and vigour, the sauvignon svelte fruitiness of grip and style. Selected stores only.

Hardys Banrock Station Chenin/Semillon/ Chardonnay 1996 14.5 C

Most uncommonly Europeanised Aussie vino. A combination of the sauciest muscadet of yesteryear with the minerality of a Loire white, and then it finishes with something of an echo of the southern Rhone. An excellent fish wine.

Hill-Smith Estate Chardonnay 1994 14 D

Jacob's Creek Chardonnay 1996 14 C

It still rates well – in spite of sailing perilously close to a fiver.

Jacob's Creek Dry Riesling 1996 14 C

Curious soft fruit with a hint of spice. Excellent summer aperitif.

Jacob's Creek Semillon/Chardonnay 1996 13 C

Lindemans Bin 65 Chardonnay 1996 15.5 C

Elegant, purposeful, balanced, finely wrought and handsomely textured. A textbook Aussie chardonnay.

Lindemans Cawarra Colombard/ Chardonnay 1996 13 C

Good but lacks pizzazz. Rather demure on the finish. Selected stores.

Lindemans Cawarra Semillon/Chardonnay 1995 15 C

The fruit has warmth, style and flavour. It is in cahoots with crisp acidity. The result is balance, personality and food compatibility. Selected stores.

Lindemans Cawarra Unoaked Chardonnay 1996 13.5 C

Selected stores.

Lindemans Padthaway Chardonnay 1994 15 E

Mick Morris Liqueur Muscat, Rutherglen (half bottle) 15.5 C

Mount Hurtle Sauvignon Blanc 1996 15.5 D

Fresh, gripping, classic, clean, deliciously fruity – this is fine stuff. Top twenty-five stores only.

Penfolds Koonunga Hill Chardonnay 1996 15.5 C

Best vintage for years: aromatic, rich, balanced, food-friendly.

Penfolds Koonunga Hill Semillon/Sauvignon Blanc 1996 15.5 C

One of the best vintages ever from Koonunga Hill: rich melon fruit, nicely crafted, with pert citric acidity. A balanced wine, soundly priced.

Penfolds Rawsons Retreat Bin 21 Semillon/Chardonnay/Colombard 1996 15 C

Richly textured, warmly fruity (some complexity on the finish where the acidity is most pertinent), this is an excellent vintage for this wine.

Penfolds The Valleys Chardonnay, South Australia 1994 16 D

Expensive but hugely expressive. It declaims with style, with tonal complexity and what it says is simple: you want total luxury, you pay for it. It's worth paying.

Rosemount Estate Diamond Label Chardonnay 1996 15.5 D

Opulence vinified. Rather grand fruit, proud and rich.

Rosemount Show Reserve Chardonnay 1995 16 E

One of Australia's most incisively fruity chardonnays, with huge hints of class, depth, balance and persistence. Expensive but very fine. Selected stores.

Sainsbury's Australian White Wine Box (3-litre box) 12 F

Tarrawingee Riesling/Gewurztraminer, Sainsbury's 14 C

Wynns Coonawarra Chardonnay 1993 14 D

Wynns Coonawarra Riesling 1996 14.5 C

Brilliant food wine (fish, chicken, Thai food) which is rich and fresh now but will develop well in bottle for two years. Selected stores.

AUSTRIAN WINE WHITE

Lenz Moser Selection Gruner Veltliner 1995  

BULGARIAN WINE RED

Bulgarian Cabernet Sauvignon 1995, Oak Aged, Russe Region, Sainsbury's 14.5 B

A soft, juicy cabernet with a touch of jam on the finish. Very fresh and perky.

Bulgarian Cabernet Sauvignon, Sainsbury's (3-litre box) 15.5 F

Young fruit with lots of vim and gusto allied to polished, smooth depth of flavour which is both intense, gluggable, and very good with food. A delicious clean red.

Bulgarian Reserve Merlot, Lovico Suhindol 1992 15 C

Rich merlot with a hint of apple-skin. Touch of spice, too.

Bulgarian Vintners Yantra Valley Cabernet Sauvignon 1990 15.5 B

Cabernet Sauvignon/Merlot, Liubimetz NV, Sainsbury's 14.5 B

A characterful wine of glugging simplicity but with an undertone which hints at complexity and depth if not altogether providing it full-throatedly.

Country Red Russe Cabernet Sauvignon/ Cinsault, Sainsbury's (1.5 litres) 15.5 D

Domaine Boyar Cabernet Sauvignon, Iambol 1992 16 C

Elegant, very stylish, rich-edged with perfectly integrated fruit/tannin/acid and a lingering finish. £3.69? Absurd!

Domaine Boyar Reserve Cabernet Sauvignon, Iambol 1992 16 C

Real class in a glass here. The texture is mouth-watering, let alone the aroma and the fruit (warm and cassis-like).

Domaine Boyar Special Reserve Cabernet Sauvignon, Iambol 1991 17 C

Magnificent price for such elegant fruit. It has a smokiness yet rich, character-filled depth of tone which is of a very high quality indeed. Utterly deliciously drinkable, yet complex. Top seventy stores.

Domaine Boyar Special Reserve Cabernet Sauvignon, Suhindol 1991 16 C

Bigger and juicier than many of its compatriots, this has richness but also an echo of real, old-style cabernet depth and the result is very impressive. Top seventy stores.

Domaine Boyar Vintage Blend Oriachovitza Merlot & Cabernet Sauvignon Reserve 1992 15 C

Superbly approachable fruit with hints of herbiness to the dryness.

JS Bulgarian Merlot, Oak Aged, Rousse 13.5 B

Glugging merlot, pure and simple.

BULGARIAN WINE — WHITE

Domaine Boyar Barrel Fermented Chardonnay, Slaviantzi 1995 11 B

CHILEAN WINE — RED

Caliterra Cabernet Sauvignon 1995 16.5 C

The complexity and the texture suggest a wine costing ten times as much. The depth, the richness, the rich chocolate finish and soft fruit are delicious beyond words. Top seventy stores.

Chilean Cabernet Sauvignon/Merlot, Sainsbury's 15.5 B

Chilean Merlot, Sainsbury's 14 C

Concha y Toro Casillero del Diablo Cabernet Sauvignon 1994  

Juicy and then it whacks you softly and seductively with rich fruit. Selected stores.

Concha y Toro Casillero del Diablo Merlot 1995  C

A most approachably gluggable merlot, no nasty edges to negotiate, which is soft and rich to finish. Top seventy stores.

Mont Gras Cabernet Sauvignon Reserva 1995 

Catering chocolate, raspberry and cassis combine to cause the instincts to say 'No, not another glass,' but you cannot resist such rich complexity. Top twenty-five stores.

Mont Gras Merlot Reserva 1995 

Brilliancy of texture, flavour, balance and sheer style. A trifle ruffled (easily) with rich food, it is soothing company with roast fowl, plain. Selected stores.

Santa Carolina Merlot Reserva, Maipo Valley 1993 

Santa Rita 120 Pinot Noir, Casablanca 1995 

Hints of farmyard and wild raspberry as you smell the wine lead to soft, rich fruit of flavour and real pinot depth. Selected stores.

Valdivieso Cabernet Sauvignon, Lontue 1996  

What a price for such vivacious complexity and youth! The

quality of the fruit and the winemaking is world-class. The flourish, the cheek, of the wine is incredible. A magnificent, rich, chewy finish of spicy cassis!

Valdivieso Cabernet Sauvignon Reserve 1995 17 D

Savoury, rich, beautifully integrated tannins and fruit, and such finesse controlling the power! This is a tremendously well-flavoured wine. Top twenty-five stores.

Valdivieso Merlot, Lontue 1996 16.5 C

A delicious merlot, no mistake, which begins juicy and ripe and then turns seriously complex and clinging. Huge clash of flavours here: spiced damsons. Top seventy stores.

Villa Montes Oak-Aged Cabernet Sauvignon Gran Reserva, Curico 1992 15 D

Mature yet sprightly and poised as it dances with plummy nicety over the tastebuds. Top seventy stores.

CHILEAN WINE WHITE

Casablanca Barrel Fermented Chardonnay, Santa Isabel Estate 1995

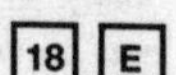

Expensive but very fine. Beautifully woody fruit with controlled white burgundy-style vegetality but the fruit is so rich, textured, complex and deep it seems never to depart the tastebuds. Top twenty-five stores.

Casablanca Chardonnay 1996 16.5 D

The combination of elements in a wine this good, at such a reasonable price, must have other chardonnay growers tearing their hair out. It is fruity yet elegant, fresh but complex, rich yet delicate. Selected stores.

Chilean Chardonnay, Sainsbury's 14 C

Muted on the finish but certainly rates as a worthy wine upfront.

Chilean Sauvignon Blanc, Sainsbury's 15.5 C

Crisp, flavourful, beautifully balanced, effortlessly classy.

Concha y Toro Casillero del Diablo Sauvignon Blanc 1995 15 C

Clean yet with hints of richness. Terrific freshness of approach. Selected stores.

Concha y Toro Marques de Casa Chardonnay 1995 17.5 D

Oily, rich as Croesus, with hints of nuts, melon and lemon so finely knitted it brings tears to your eyes. A beautiful wine. Selected stores.

Santa Carolina Chardonnay, Lontue 1996 17 

A hugely seductive aroma, superb texture to the rich fruit and a vivid, lingering finish. Ripe, complex, youthful yet mature, this is a world-class wine. Top seventy stores only.

Santa Rita Chardonnay, Estate Reserve 1996 16 D

A cool chardonnay, not overblown or too ripe. Has crispness and tone, and a citric undertone. Selected stores.

ENGLISH WINE — WHITE

Denbies Estate English Table Wine, 1992 10 C

Lamberhurst Sovereign Medium Dry 10 B

FRENCH WINE — RED

Antonin Rodet Gevrey Chambertin 1994 10 G

Vastly underfruited. Hugely overpriced. Top sixty stores.

Beaujolais, Sainsbury's 12 C

Beaujolais-Villages, Les Roches Grillees 1995 12 C

Bordeaux Rouge, Sainsbury's 14.5 B

Brilliantly priced claret of some class. Dry and flavourful.

Bush Vine Grenache, Coteaux du Languedoc 1995 14 C

Cabernet Sauvignon Syrah VdP d'Oc, Sainsbury's 14 B

Cabernet Sauvignon VdP d'Oc, Sainsbury's 14 C

Chateau Barreyres Haut Medoc 1991 14.5 D

Classic pong on the nose of manure, boot polish and cracked

leather, dry tannic fruit of charm, and a faint vigour on the finish. For purists only. Top seventy-three stores.

Chateau Belgrave Grand Cru Classe Haut Medoc 1994 11 G

Meaty aroma, brisk tannins overlaying peppery cabernet and hints of leather (from, I guess, merlot). However, this is just an impression. The tannins soon gobble the fruit, in an hour of opening, and so it's witless with food.

Chateau Beychevelle, 4e Cru Classe St Julien 1991 14 G

Chateau Calon-Segur Grand Cru Classe St Estephe 1993 15 G

Rich, chocolatey, well-evolved, tannicky, Calon-Segur has always drunk well young. This has richness, no coarse tannins, firm texture, a whiff of Medoc classiness. Will last for five to seven years but improve for only three more. Not at all stores.

Chateau Coutelin-Merville St Estephe 1990 14 F

Chateau d'Aigueville Cotes du Rhone 1995 13 C

Chateau de la Tour, Bordeaux Rouge 1994 14 D

Chateau de Peyrat Premieres Cotes de Bordeaux 1994 13 D

Tries hard.

Chateau de Rully Rouge, Rodet 1993 12 E

Chateau Ferriere 3e Cru Margaux 1993 13 G

Vastly overpriced. Top twenty stores.

Chateau la Louviere, Pessac-Leognan 1993

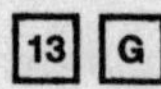

Chateau La Vieille Cure, Fronsac 1990 17 E

Sainsbury's deliberately held back stocks of this 1990 (selling '92 and '93 ahead of it) and the result is a superbly mature claret of perfect weight and balance. Lovely soft tannins and very rich delivery to the throat. Top seventy stores.

Chateau Lanessan, Haut Medoc 1989 14 F

Expensive but smoothly arrogant and well textured. Top forty-four stores only.

Chateau Lynch Bages, 5e Cru Classe Pauillac 1991 14.5 G

Chateau Marquis de Terme, 4e Cru Classe Margaux 1992 13 F

Chateau Marsau, Cotes de Francs 1995 15 D

Touch light but lots of dry, tannic fruit upfront and a lovely herby finish. Excellent with food. Selected stores.

Chateau Pavie Macquin Grand Cru Classe Saint Emilion 1992 14.5 G

Ludicrous amount of money to pay for a bottle of wine unless the stuff courses down your veins and sets your cuticles alight. This one gets about as far as the elbow. Not at all stores.

Chateau Segonzac Premieres Cotes de Blaye Bordeaux 1994 14.5 D

Rich, very dry, hugely full of development potential over the next five years or so.

Chateau Tassin, Sichel Bordeaux Rouge 1995 14.5 C

A simple glugging claret on one level but it hints at greater depth than this and the finish is profound. Good value here. Selected stores.

Chateauneuf du Pape Les Galets Blancs 1994 14 E

Dry, herby, rich, good impactful tannins. Selected stores.

Claret Cuvee Prestige, Sainsbury's 13.5 C

Classic Selection Margaux 1993, Sainsbury's 13 D

Classic Selection Saint Emilion 1993, Sainsbury's 14 E

At last! A Classic Selection wine which fits the category! (Little expensive though.) Humph! Top seventy stores only.

Clos Magne Figeac, Saint Emilion 1993 16 E

Serious cedar wood aroma invites you in and then doesn't disappoint as you relax in the very richly endowed fruit which offers beautifully smooth tannic/acid balance. This wine is improving well in bottle. Top 150 stores.

Comte de Signargues Cotes du Rhone Villages 1994 14 D

Interesting double-faced wine of seeming fruity lightness but it packs a dry tannic wallop on the finish. Selected stores.

Corbieres, Sainsbury's (3-litre box) 13.5 F

Crozes-Hermitage Les Jalets, Jaboulet Aine 1994 14.5 E

Surprisingly forward, ripe and ready. Only hints of earth and bramble. Possibly 16.5 in three to four years' time.

Cuvee Prestige Cotes du Rhone, Sainsbury's 13 C

Domaine de Sours Bordeaux Rouge 1993 12.5 C

Domaine du Pujol Minervois, Cave de la Cessane 1995 16.5 C

What a delightful wine! It is the essence of drinkability and food-compatibility: dry, rich, characterful, gorgeous. Not at all stores.

Domaine Rio Magno Pinot Noir, VdP l'Ile de Beaute 1994 12 C

Fleurie La Madone, 1995 13 E

Gigondas Tour de Queyron 1992 16 D

Expensive, but it shows how elegant those rich, herby, warm, blood-arousing southern Rhones can be. This has insouciant class and quiet stylishness – it doesn't quite have the raucous impactfulness of some of its louder brethren.

Hermitage Monier de 'La Sizeranne' 1991 14.5 G

Julienas Chateau des Capitans 1995 11 D

Light but not fantastic. Selected stores.

La Baume Cabernet Sauvignon, VdP d'Oc 1994, Sainsbury's 16 C

Dry, rich, gently peppery and deep – this is class cabernet.

La Baume Merlot, VdP d'Oc 1994, Sainsbury's 15.5 C

Soft, subtle, chocolate edge. Has fullness and depth and lovely texture.

La Baume Merlot/Cabernet Sauvignon 1995 15 C

Soft, warm, prettily alert on the tongue with its textured herbiness and hugely savoury finish. Delightful.

La Baume Syrah VdP d'Oc 1995, Sainsbury's 16 C

Invigorating blend of controlled rusticity (Old World) and velvet incisiveness (New World). Terrific glugging here.

La Source de Vignelaure 1994 14 C

Le Second Vin de Mouton Rothschild, Pauillac 1993 10 H

An expensive joke played on asses' heads.

Merlot Bankside Gallery, VdP d'Oc 1995 16.5 C

Chocolatey, thick, beautiful textured tannins integrated with the fruit. This is a class merlot of stunning quality for the money. Selected stores.

Minervois, Sainsbury's 13 B

Morey St Denis Premier Cru Domaine des Lambrays 1992 13.5 G

Some classic hints of old-style burgundy here: farmyard muck and truffles.

Moulin a Vent, Cave Kuhnel 1994 10 E

Nuits St-Georges 'Aux Meurgers' Domaine Bertagna 1994 10 G

If one's aspiration is ditchwater, this bottle is ascendant. For the common-sense tippler, however, £15 for this dull wine is sheer effrontery.

Red Burgundy, Sainsbury's 13 D

Has some character, but I'm not so sure I like the price.

Saint Joseph, Prieure Beaulieu 1991 13 D

Selection Peter A Sichel Oak Matured Bordeaux 1994 13 C

Soft and fruity. Very drinkable. Selected stores.

St Joseph Le Grand Pompee, Jaboulet Ainee 1994 13.5 E

A lot of money for a Rhone of uneasy texture and somewhat moody fruit. Top seventy stores.

Vacqueyras Brotte 1993 16.5 D

Has a texture of high class, fruit of great depth, and a finish which reminds the romantic of herb-scented evenings in northern Provence. Delicious! Top seventy stores.

Valreas Domaine de la Grande Bellane 1995 (Organic) 14.5 D

Has character, bite, depth and personality. Dry but fully operational in the fruit department, this is solid food wine of richness and style. Selected stores.

Vin de Pays de l'Ardeche, Sainsbury's 13.5 B

Vin de Pays de l'Aude Rouge, Sainsbury's 16 B

Remarkable character and wisdom in a wine so young, chirpy and cheap. Has depth and richness, properly modulated, and an integrated earthy edge. Dry, decisive, daring.

Vin de Pays de la Cite de Carcassonne Merlot 1995, Sainsbury's 14 C

Vin de Pays des Bouches du Rhone, Sainsbury's 13.5 B

Juicy, friendly, fun with pasta.

Vin Rouge de France Dry Red Wine, Sainsbury's (3-litre box) 12 B

Fairly ordinary stuff. Better chilled, with a summer barbecue.

Vosne Romanee 'Les Beaumonts' Domaine Bertagna 1994 10 G

Top nineteen stores.

Vougeot Clos Bertagna 1994 9 G

Total waste of space on Sainsbury's shelves. Selected stores.

FRENCH WINE WHITE

Alsace Gewurztraminer Sainsbury's 14 D

Rich, almost cloyingly so, with a scent of crushed rose-petals and a spiciness on the fruit. Very musky, thick stuff. Selected stores.

Blanc Anjou Medium Dry, Sainsbury's 12 B

Bordeaux Blanc Cuvee Prestige, Sainsbury's 11 C

Bordeaux Blanc, Sainsbury's 12 C

Bourgogne Chardonnay Reserve Personelle, Oak Aged, Laroche 1994 14 D

Good texture and firm fruit. Good with chicken dishes. It does have some quiet vegetal complexity which stands up to food. Top seventy stores.

Chablis 1er Cru Montee de Tonnerre, Brocard 1993 13.5 E

Chablis Premier Cru Les Vaillons, Paul Dugenais 1994 10 E

Selected stores.

Chardonnay Bankside Gallery, VdP d'Oc 1995 15.5 C

Elegant, classy, stylish, balanced, sanely priced. Selected stores.

Chardonnay VdP d'Oc, Sainsbury's (3-litre box) 12.5 G

Chateau l'Ortolan Bordeaux Blanc 1995 15.5 C

It's a long time since I last tasted a bordeaux blanc under a fiver which had real texture (plump and rich), real fruit (melony), and incisive acidity. An excellent shellfish wine.

Classic Selection Muscadet de Sevre et Maine Sur Lie 1995, Sainsbury's 12.5 D

Not bad, not great. But overpriced and still muscadet. Selected stores.

Classic Selection Pouilly Fuisse 1995, Sainsbury's 12 E

Selected stores.

Cotes du Luberon Blanc, Sainsbury's 13.5 B

Country plonking. Fruity after a fashion, faintly earthy. Selected stores.

Domaine de Grandchamp Sauvignon Blanc, Bergerac 1996 14 D

At the rich end of sauvignons. Not grassy or lean but fruit with a crisp echo only. Selected stores.

Domaine de la Tuilerie Merlot Rose, 1995 14 C

Gaillac Blanc, Sainsbury's 15 C

Grenache Rose VdP de l'Ardeche, Sainsbury's 12 B

La Baume Chardonnay, VdP d'Oc 1995, Sainsbury's 16.5 C

Magnificent cool class. Sheer satin, deep fruit (but never blowsy or over-ripe), this is a high-class act at a great price.

La Baume Sauvignon Blanc, VdP d'Oc 1995, Sainsbury's 16.5 C

Super texture, rolling and rich, with flavour, style, class and depth. A classic sauvignon. Better than a hundred sancerres at twice the price.

Louis Alexandre Chablis 1995 11 E

Macon Blanc Villages, Domaine les Chenevieres 1995 13.5 

Not bad as white burgundies go, but at nigh on six quid *please* can I have more fruit? Is it asking so much?

Menetou Salon Domaine Henri Pelle 1996 14 D

Crisp, impishly fruity and classily gooseberryish. Selected stores.

Meursault 1er Cru Les Charmes 1992 10 G

An inexpressibly insignificant level of fruit for a significant level of dosh.

Meursault 'Sous la Velle', Mestre-Michelot 1994 10 G

Ludicrous – how do these Burgundians get away with selling this boring, overpriced junk to a professional supermarket wine-buyer?

Moulin des Groyes, Cotes de Duras Blanc 1995 13.5 C

This is one of those wines which taste wonderful sipped in the summer sun in a cafe a few hundred yards from the vineyard. Travel seems to make it coy and uncommunicative.

Mouton Cadet Bordeaux Blanc 1994 12 D

Muscadet de Sevre et Maine, Sainsbury's (3-litre box) 13 F

Muscat de Beaumes de Venise, Sainsbury's (half bottle) 14 C

Muscat de Mireval, Domaine du Mas Neuf 1994 (half bottle) 14.5 D

A lovely, gently honeyed wine with a hint of mineralised acidity to the richness. So it works well with blue cheese or for the solo drinker with a sweet tooth and a book. Top seventy stores.

Premieres Cotes de Bordeaux, Sainsbury's 13 C

Sweet but not cloying, it makes a pleasant aperitif, chilled, in summer. Selected stores.

Puligny-Montrachet 1er Cru, Hameau de Blagny 1993 10 G

A perfectly drinkable £3.50 bottle of wine. An undrinkable bottle at £19.95 – no one in their senses will swallow that price tag with this respectable rather than exciting level of fruit. Top nineteen stores.

Reserve Saint Marc, Sauvignon Blanc VdP d'Oc 1996 14 C

Refined but with an impudently fruity finish. Not at all stores.

Riesling Schoenenburg Grand Cru de Riquewihr, Dopff au Moulin 1993 15 F

Very rich and ripe, potently so, with a hint of grapefruit on the finish. A lush, exotic beauty of great charm and persistence. Will develop for two to three years. Top twenty-five stores.

Sauvignon de St Bris, Bersan 1995, Sainsbury's 13.5 D

Sichel Selection Graves Blanc 1995 14 C

Has an imposing, somewhat cosy, level of fat fruit but not entirely a concomitant level of balancing acidity. It seems overstuffed as a result but is classy, good for rich seafood dishes with ravishing sauces, and not obscenely priced.

Tokay Pinot Gris Reserve, Dopff au Moulin 1994 14 D

Delicious apricot fruit which will develop more complexity if kept for three years and rate 17 points. Top seventy stores.

Touraine Sauvignon Blanc, Sainsbury's 10 B

Vin Blanc de France Dry White Wine, Sainsbury's (3-litre box) 11 B

Vin Blanc Medium Dry, Sainsbury's 12.5 B

Vin de Pays de l'Aude Blanc, Sainsbury's 14 B

Simple, fruity, crisp, well-managed. Good fruit, good price, terrific little glug or with fish.

Vin de Pays des Cotes de Gascogne, Domaine Bordes 1995 15 C

White Burgundy, Sainsbury's 13.5 D

A thoroughly decent white burgundy of some style.

GERMAN WINE WHITE

Baden Gewurztraminer 1995 12 C

Interesting, if not as expressive as the Alsatian version. Pricey for the style, too.

Bereich Bernkastel, Sainsbury's 11 B

Bernkasteler Badstube Riesling Spatlese Von Kesselstatt 1988 14 D

Blue Nun Liebfraumilch 13 C

Not as yucky as most Liebs but pricier than comparable, forwardly-fruity off-dry wines from elsewhere. Decent aperitif in summer. Selected stores.

Dexheimer Doktor Spatlese 1994, Sainsbury's 15 C

Erdener Treppchen, Riesling Spatlese 1985 12 D

Hock, Sainsbury's 10 A

Liebfraumilch, Sainsbury's 10 B

Mainzer St Alban Auslese, Rheinhessen 1994 14 C

Delicious honeyed, smoky edge. Great with fresh fruit and goat's cheese. Top seventy stores.

Mainzer St Alban Kabinett, Rheinhessen 1995 13 C

Amusing aperitif. Won't shock your guests or thrill them but it might tickle them.

Mainzer St Alban Spatlese, Rheinhessen 1994 13.5 C

This has a sweet tone but is far from a honeyed dessert style. Best as a palate-arouser, I think. Selected stores.

Mosel, Sainsbury's 12 B

Niersteiner Gutes Domtal, Sainsbury's 11 B

Oppenheimer Krotenbrunnen Kabinett, Sainsbury's 12 B

Palatinarum Riesling, Zimmerman Graeff 1995 12.5 C

Rather expensive for the simplicity of the lemony fruit. Nice with grilled prawns, though. Top seventy stores.

Palatinarum Rivaner, Zimmerman Graeff 1995 13 C

Selected stores.

Piesporter Michelsberg, Sainsbury's 12 B

Weisenheimer Mandelgarten Ortega Trockenbeerenauslese 1994 15 E

GREEK WINE RED

Kourtakis VdP de Crete Red 14 B

Earthy, drinkable, food-friendly, well fruited. Fun yet will work with a beef casserole. Selected stores.

GREEK WINE WHITE

Kourtakis VdP de Crete White 12.5 B

Retsina, Sainsbury's 14 B

Old cricket bats soaked in fruit juice. Has a certain devil-may-care freshness. Needs Greek food to be friendly.

HUNGARIAN WINE RED

River Route Merlot 1994 14 C

Aromatic, ripe, very giving, nice leathery aftertaste. A creditable merlot at a very low price.

HUNGARIAN WINE WHITE

Chapel Hill Estate Chardonnay Barrique Aged 1995

Excellent ripe fruit with an edge of pineapple and citrus. Suffers, at this price, from comparison with richer Chileans but there's no denying its class. Selected stores.

Gyongyos Estate Sauvignon Blanc 1995

Hungarian Irsai Oliver, Sainsbury's

Hungarian Zenit, Nagyrede Estate 1995

Tokay 5-Puttonyos 1988

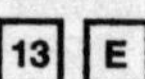

I find this over-priced and too medicinal in character. With a streaming cold, and in bed, it might prove congenial.

ITALIAN WINE RED

Barrique Aged Cabernet Sauvignon Atesino 1995

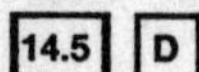

Touch green and peppery but will soften and develop well over the summer. Brilliant with food with its concentrated blackcurrant.

Campomarino Biferno 1994 15.5 C

Lovely vigour here stemmed in its rush to please by the undertone of herby dryness. A really classic Italian red of savour and style – brilliant with food.

Castelgreve Chianti Classico Riserva 1991 15.5 D

Chianti 1994, Sainsbury's 14 C

Chianti Classico, Badia a Passignano, Antinori 1994 15 D

Perfect Tuscan baked richness (not coarse) and depth. Lovely texture and style. Top seventy stores.

Chianti Classico, Briante 1994 15 D

Copertino Riserva 1992, Sainsbury's 13.5 B

Juicy, light, rather coy wine.

Cortegiara Amarone della Valpolicella Classico, Allegrini 1991 15 E

Apples and cherries to smell, it turns juicy and then rich and roasted as it descends. Magical effect on the arteries, this wine – really summons up the blood! Top seventy stores.

Lambrusco Rosso, Sainsbury's 12 B

Lambrusco Secco Rosso 'Vecchia-Modena' 14 B

Merlot Corvina Vino da Tavola del Veneto, Sainsbury's 14.5 B

Montepulciano d'Abruzzo, Sainsbury's 15 B

Negroamaro del Salento 14 B

Rosso delle Venezie, Sainsbury's (3-litre box) 13.5 F

Simple cherry-edged fruit. Selected stores.

Rosso di Verona, Sainsbury's 11 B

Sangiovese di Romagna, Sainsbury's 13.5 B

Sangiovese di Toscana, Cecchi 13.5 C

Sicilian Nero d'Avola & Merlot, Sainsbury's 15 C

Sicilian Red, Sainsbury's 14 B

The essence of dry yet fruity, simple yet flavourful, everyday swigging wine.

Squinzano Mottura 1994 14 B

Selected stores.

Teroldego Rotaliano Geoff Merrill, Sainsbury's 12 C

Selected stores.

Valpolicella, Sainsbury's 11.5 B

Vino Nobile di Montepulciano, Cecchi 1991 14 D

ITALIAN WINE — WHITE

Barrique Aged Chardonnay Atesino 1994 15 C

Delicious underlying richness and flavour to the freshness.

Bianco di Custoza, Geoff Merrill 1995 14 C

Bianco di Verona, Sainsbury's 13 B

Chardonnay del Salento Vigneto di Caramia 1996 15.5 D

One of the classiest southern Italian chardonnays around: rich, giving, textured, ripe but not rampant, it's silky and quite delicious. Selected stores.

Cortese del Piemonte 1995 15 C

Garganega Vino da Tavola del Veneto, Sainsbury's 13.5 B

Inzolia & Chardonnay (Sicily), Sainsbury's 14 C

Lambrusco Bianco Medium Sweet, Sainsbury's 10 B

Lambrusco Rosato, Sainsbury's 10 B

Lambrusco Secco, Sainsbury's 8 B

Le Trulle Chardonnay del Salento 1996 15.5 C

Delicious, gentle, rich, smooth and very well-balanced. Top 100 stores only.

Soave, Sainsbury's 11 B

Trebbiano di Romagna, Sainsbury's 14.5 B

Tuscan White, Cecchi 13 B

Verdicchio dei Castelli di Jesi Classico 1995, Sainsbury's 14 C

Charm, style and crisply cut fruit make a fine specimen out of an oft-despised breed.

LEBANESE WINE RED

Chateau Musar 1989 12 E

Looks and smells like a light game and mushroom sauce. The fruit is creaky and sweet – a touch toothless. Top ninety stores.

NEW ZEALAND WINE WHITE

Matua Eastern Bays Chardonnay 1995 15 D

An idiosyncratic chardonnay of aroma and weight. Has soft fruit with a nutty undertone and a delicious smoky finish. Top ninety stores.

Matua Pinot Gris 1995 15 D

Marlborough, having stupefied the wine world with its rapier-keen sauvignon blanc, turns its attention to pinot gris. Certain Italian wine growers may feel a distinct chill here. This wine is nutty, fresh and very elegant.

Montana Sauvignon Blanc, Marlborough 1996 14.5 D

More grassy and fresh than previous vintages. Typical Marlborough fruit – a solid example.

New Zealand Dry White, Sainsbury's 15 C

An echo of grassiness on the dry honey melon fruit. A comfortable white wine of charm and easy drinking.

New Zealand Medium White, Sainsbury's 12 C

Selected stores.

Nobilo White Cloud 1996 13 C

The Sanctuary Sauvignon Blanc, Marlborough 1996 15.5 D

Nettly and grassy to smell – a scent picked up by the whistle-clean fruit. An elegant, typical Kiwi wine of style and class. Great with shellfish. Selected stores.

Villa Maria Private Bin Chardonnay, Marlborough 1996 13.5 D

Falls a little short of what a six-quid-plus chardonnay should be.

Villa Maria Private Bin Sauvignon Blanc, Marlborough 1996 15 D

Delicate grassy notes to the richly restrained fruit. Elegantly and finely cut.

PORTUGUESE WINE RED

Cabernet Sauvignon Ribatejo, Sainsbury's 13 C

Do Campo Tinto, Sainsbury's 14.5 B

Portuguese Red Wine, Sainsbury's 13 B

PORTUGUESE WINE WHITE

Do Campo Branco Peter Bright, Sainsbury's 14 B

Do Campo Rosado, Sainsbury's 12 B

Portuguese Rose, Sainsbury's 8 B

Santa Sara Barrel Fermented Reserve 1995 16 C

Complex, exciting, rich (layers of melon with a nutty overcoat), beautifully textured, warm, full and fruity yet very elegant. Terrific tipple. Top eighty-five stores only.

Sauvignon Blanc Ribatejo 1995, Sainsbury's 15.5 C

Smoky, rich, deep, utterly deliciously priced. This is a terrific wine for the money. Excellent with fish and chicken dishes.

Sauvignon Blanc Rueda, Lurton 14 C

A lovely texture of calm, quiet, understated richness. Delicious fish wine. Selected stores.

Vinho Verde, Sainsbury's 12 B

ROMANIAN WINE RED

Romanian Pinot Noir Dealul Mare, Sainsbury's 14.5 B

SOUTH AFRICAN WINE RED

Bellingham Cabernet Sauvignon, Paarl 1994 14 D

Bellingham Merlot 1995 14 C

More like a cabernet than a merlot, with a juicy finish. Selected stores.

Fairview Cabernet Sauvignon, Paarl 1995 15 D

The usual high-class act from this estate, though I tend to feel this cabernet is more of a glugger than previous vintages. The texture is soft, the fruit aromatic and gently rich.

Fairview Pinotage, Paarl 1995 17 C

Baked-biscuit fruit of great richness, fruitinesss, charm, superb texture and great depth. Lovely flavour here which you feel you could drink for ever. Top seventy stores.

Neil Ellis Cabernet Sauvignon/Merlot 1994 13 E

Tries hard to be a claret taste-alike and succeeds! Dry, expensive, rather austere. Top twenty-six stores.

South African Cape Red Wine, Sainsbury's 13.5 B

South African Pinot Noir Reserve Selection 1995, Sainsbury's 12 C

South African Pinotage Reserve Selection 1995, Sainsbury's 15.5 C

South African Pinotage, Sainsbury's 14 C

South African Reserve Selection Merlot 1995, Sainsbury's 16 D

Superbly gripping structure which is soft, gently leathery, firm yet very supple. A beautifully textured, dry wine of some class. Top seventy stores.

South African Ruby Cabernet/Cinsault, Sainsbury's 14 C

Soft, almost soppy, frisky as a young pup and huge fun to slurp with friends. Top seventy stores.

Swartland Cinsault 1996 15.5 B

Cheap and so cheerful besides, it's wonderful. Has depth, richness, flavour and a haunting warmth on the finish which is quite delicious. Selected stores.

Vergelegen Cabernet Sauvignon, Stellenbosch 1995 16.5 D

This creeps stealthily and deliciously insidiously from nose to throat like some richly exotic secret agent of Bacchus determined to titillate but only at the finish produces its finest, mysterious, rich, enigmatic moment. Its flavour lingers like a wanted guest. Top twenty-five stores only.

Vergelegen Merlot 1994

Lot of money but a lot of wine. Has an exotic dark beauty of tone about the leathery, cassis-touched fruit which is dry, profound and very classy. Top ten stores.

SOUTH AFRICAN WINE — WHITE

Boschendal Chardonnay, Paarl 1994 12.5 D

Cape Dry White Wine, Sainsbury's 14 B

Cape Medium White Wine, Sainsbury's 14 B

South African Chardonnay, Western Cape, Sainsbury's 15 C

Riches for the tongue but not poverty for the pocket. A well-balanced wine of flavour and style at a very good price.

South African Colombard, Sainsbury's 14 B

South African Fume Blanc Reserve, Robertson 1996, Sainsbury's 14 D

Delicate yet incisive, classy yet not beyond mucking in with fish dishes. Selected stores.

South African Sauvignon Blanc, Sainsbury's 13 B

South African Sauvignon Blanc/ Chardonnay, Sainsbury's 15 C

Thelema Sauvignon Blanc 1995 15.5 E

Vergelegen Chardonnay 1995 15.5 D

Very classy stuff. Lovely controlled use of wood, fine depth of fruit, complex structure. A delicious bottle of wine at a fair price. Top twenty-five stores.

Vergelegen Chardonnay Reserve 1995 13 E

Expensive and not as good as the same estate's non-reserve chardonnay. Top ten stores.

Vergelegen Sauvignon Blanc, Stellenbosch 1996 15 D

Calm, fresh, elegant, subtle, finely balanced. Top twenty-five stores.

SPANISH WINE RED

Classic Selection Rioja Reserva 1990, Sainsbury's 14 E

Rich, dry, personable, this is good company for a meat dish – though I'm uncomfortable with £7.45 for such a wine.

El Conde Oak-Aged Vino da Mesa, Sainsbury's 14 B

JS Rioja Crianza Bodegas Olarra 1993 14 C

Jumilla, Sainsbury's

Brilliant on-form wine of jammy drinkability and rich, tonally complete structure which allows the wine to finish with a great hearty flourish of fruit. Terrific value and quaffability with food versatility.

Navarra, Sainsbury's

What fantastic value! Real rich, classy fruit shrouded in dryness.

Navarra Tempranillo/Cabernet Sauvignon Crianza 1994, Sainsbury's

Beauteous texture of ruffled velvet and this, with the aroma and the depth of fruit, makes for a remarkably stylish wine for the money.

Orobio Rioja Reserva 1990

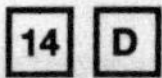

Rioja Reserva Vina Ardanza 1989

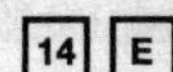

Expensive, very expensive. Top forty stores.

Santara Cabernet Merlot, Conca de Barbera 1994

Develops licorice and dry herb flavours as it opens up on the tastebuds. Certainly as mature as it needs to be, the wine has an opulence, a flippant depth of richness and a wonderful savoury finish. Superb value for money.

Valencia Oak Aged, Sainsbury's

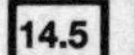

Quite delicious. It begins brisk and dry, then turns really rich and compellingly gluggable.

Marques de Caceres Rioja Blanco Crianza 1993 — 13 C

SPANISH WINE — WHITE

Navarra Blanco, Sainsbury's — 14 B

Santara Chardonnay 1995 — 16.5 C

This is one of the very few chardonnays under four quid which gives Chile a run for the same money: rich, perfectly developed, complex, utterly delicious. It has plot, character and wit. It's a literary gem.

USA WINE — RED

California Red, Sainsbury's — 13 B

E & J Gallo Turning Leaf Cabernet Sauvignon 1994 — 13.5 D

E & J Gallo Turning Leaf Zinfandel 1994 — 12 D

Gallo Sonoma Cabernet Sauvignon 1992 — 13.5 E

South Bay Reserve American Cabernet Sauvignon — 14 D

Love the touch of warm, tannic fruit on the finish. Real class in a glass here. Selected stores.

South Bay Vineyards American Pinot Noir 13.5 C

Classic aroma but the finish sucks.

Washington Hills Merlot, Columbia Valley 1995 16.5 D

Super, world-class merlot of a rolling, expansive richness which is gripping and rich. It has a delicate power and great depth. Soft leather and soft fruits, dryly expressed, in vivid embrace. A delicious wine. Top twenty-five stores.

USA WINE — WHITE

California White, Sainsbury's 12 B

E & J Gallo Turning Leaf Chardonnay 1994 14 D

South Bay Vineyards American Chardonnay, California 12 C

Not hugely overwhelming for a fiver.

Sutter Home White Zinfandel 1995 12 C

Washington Hills Chardonnay, Columbia Valley 1995 14.5 D

Lingering, rich, beautifully textured with lots of flavour and rich depth to it. Top thirty stores.

FORTIFIED WINE

1985 Vintage Port Quinta Dona Matilde, Sainsbury's 15 G

Very rich and soft and the sweetness is controlled and fine. Great with fruit cake and rich cheeses. Top sixty stores.

Aged Amontillado, Sainsbury's (half bottle) 14 B

Blandy's Duke of Clarence Malmsey Madeira 13 E

Cantine Pellegrino Superiore Garibaldi Dolce Marsala (half bottle) 14 D

Cream Montilla, Sainsbury's 14 B

Dow's Extra Dry White Port 14 E

Manzanilla, Sainsbury's 12 C

Matusalem Sherry (half bottle) 14 E

Medium Dry Amontillado, Sainsbury's 12 C

Medium Dry Montilla, Sainsbury's 14 B

Moscatel Pale Cream, Sainsbury's 15 C

Old Oloroso, Sainsbury's (half bottle) 14 B

Pale Cream Montilla, Sainsbury's 13 B

Pale Cream Sherry, Sainsbury's	14	C
Pale Dry Amontillado, Sainsbury's	15	C
Pale Dry Fino Sherry, Sainsbury's	15.5	C
Pale Dry Montilla, Sainsbury's	13.5	B
Palo Cortado, Sainsbury's (half bottle)	14	B
Pellegrino Marsala	14	B
Rich Cream Sherry, Sainsbury's	14.5	C
Sainsbury's 5 Year Old Sercial (half bottle)	14.5	E
Sainsbury's LBV 1989	13.5	E
Sainsbury's Ruby	13.5	D
Sainsbury's Tawny	14	D
Taylors LBV, 1989	14.5	E

SPARKLING WINE/CHAMPAGNE

Angas Brut Rose (Australia)	15	D
Asti, Sainsbury's	11	C

Blanc de Noirs Champagne Brut, Sainsbury's 14.5 F

Decidedly delicate and elegant.

Cava Rosado, Sainsbury's 15 C

Cava, Sainsbury's 16 D

Superb delicacy of tone, restrained richness, citric pertinacity and overall balance.

Champagne Alfred Gratien NV 13 G

An elegant hint-of-lemon bubbly which is rashly overpriced.

Champagne Extra Dry, Sainsbury's 13.5 G

'Delicate and elegant,' claims the front label, and who am I to argue? Though I do argue about the 'extra dry' tag.

Chardonnay Brut Methode Traditionelle, Sainsbury's (France) 14.5 D

Demi Sec Champagne, Sainsbury's 10 E

Gallo Brut 10 D

Lindauer Special Reserve 14 E

Classy and stylish. Better than many more expensive champagnes. Top seventy stores.

Madeba Brut, Robertson (South Africa) 14 D

Nice warmth to the fruit here.

Mercier Brut 11 G

Mercier Demi Sec 12 G

Sekt, Sainsbury's 11 C

Sparkling White Burgundy, Pinot Noir/Chardonnay 1992, Sainsbury's 14 D

Soft with rich hints. Has some swash to its buckle, this bubbly. Top seventy stores.

Vin Mousseux Brut, Sainsbury's 12 C

Vintage Brut, Cremant de Loire 1992, Sainsbury's 14 D

Rich and classy. Selected stores.

Yalumba Pinot Noir Chardonnay 16 E

So much tastier and better-priced than hundreds of champagnes. Selected stores.

J Sainsbury plc
Stamford House
Stamford Street
London SE1 9LL
Tel 0171 921 6000
Fax 0171 921 7925
Internet order http://www.j-sainsbury.co.uk

SOMERFIELD/ GATEWAY

ARGENTINIAN WINE — RED

Argentine Country Red San Juan, Somerfield  B

ARGENTINIAN WINE — WHITE

Argentine Country White, Somerfield 16 B

Dry, clean, modern tippling for relative peanuts. Not hugely fruity but a damn decent glug. And the plastic cork means no tree bark gumming up the flavour!

AUSTRALIAN WINE — RED

Australian Dry Red , Somerfield  B

Little cherry-ripe lad.

Australian Shiraz 13 C

Cabernet Sauvignon, Somerfield 13.5 C

Hardys Bankside Shiraz 1995 14 D

Wins on its approach, rather than its quiet departure.

Penfolds Koonunga Hill Shiraz Cabernet 1995 14 D

Very tasty, very rich. Very sparky stuff.

Penfolds Rawson's Retreat Bin 35 Cabernet/Shiraz/Ruby Cabernet 1995 13.5 C

Usual decent turnout.

Somerfield Cabernet Shiraz 13.5 C

South East Australian Cabernet Sauvignon 1995 

Mature, aromatic, brisk (i.e. some tannin on the edge of fruit which has bite) and rich, this is an excellent casserole wine.

AUSTRALIAN WINE WHITE

Hardys Nottage Hill Chardonnay 1996 14.5 C

This elegant style of Aussie chardonnay is light years ahead of the blowsy blockbusters of yesteryear.

Jacob's Creek Chardonnay 1996 14 C

It still rates well – in spite of sailing perilously close to a fiver.

Jacob's Creek Semillon Chardonnay 1996 13 C

Jamiesons Run Chardonnay 1996 14.5 E

Eight quid isn't peanuts but then peanuts do not accompany this rich wine. You need soft lights, soft music and pliant company.

Lindemans Bin 65 Chardonnay 1996 15 D

Nine pee over a fiver? Even so, it's still cutting the mustard as a brand, this wine, and in this vintage the customary satiny texture and flavour have a delicate smokiness.

Lindemans Coonawarra Botrytis Riesling 1994 16 D

A wonderfully surprising Aussie: sweet-natured, waxy, burnt-edged, rampantly rich and just great with fresh fruit, ice cream, foie gras. Or – just drink it with the Walkman reclining in a hammock. It's a lot more exotic, sexy and gorgeous than the Spice Girls. Selected stores.

Lindemans Unoaked Cawarra Chardonnay 1996 13 C

Penfolds Australian Dry White 1996, Somerfield 14 B

A fresh wine of tentative fruitiness.

Penfolds Rawsons Retreat Bin 21 Semillon/Chardonnay/Colombard 1996 15 C

Richly textured, warmly fruity (some complexity on the finish where the acidity is most pertinent), this is an excellent vintage for this wine.

Penfolds The Valley Chardonnay 1995 15 D

Packed with flavour which never intrudes rudely – only graciously.

Rosemount Estate Semillon/Chardonnay 1996 14 D

Balanced, unbashful, excellent with fish.

BULGARIAN WINE RED

Bulgarian Cabernet Sauvignon 1992, Somerfield 14 B

One of summer's bargain barbecue reds.

Country Red Merlot/Pinot Noir, Somerfield 15 B

Stambolovo Merlot Reserve 1990 16 C

Wonderful richness and maturity yet surprisingly vigorous, warm, deep and savoury.

BULGARIAN WINE WHITE

Somerfield Bulgarian Country White 14.5 B

CHILEAN WINE RED

Chilean Cabernet Sauvignon 1996, Somerfield 17 C

Soft, savoury-chocolate fruit, firmly textured, hugely gluggable.

Chilean Red Wine 1996, Somerfield 16.5 B

Dry, rich, good tannins, soft chewy texture, lingering finish.

Stowells of Chelsea Chilean Merlot Cabernet (3-litre box)  C

CHILEAN WINE — WHITE

Chilean Chardonnay 1996, Somerfield 16.5 C

Great quality of fruit handled with deftness by one of Chile's most humane crushers of grapes. A beautifully balanced, rich, purposeful, expressive chardonnay of depth and flavour. Great class here for a remarkable price.

Chilean Sauvignon Blanc 1996, Somerfield 14.5 C

Clean, fresh, touched by citrus and soft melon but undercut by a crisp acidity, this is a first-class, well-balanced wine for the money.

Chilean White Wine 1996 16.5 B

Dry, clean, fresh, nutty.

FRENCH WINE — RED

Beaujolais 1996, Somerfield 10 C

Turgid.

Bergerac Rouge 1996, Somerfield 11 B

Earthy? You could pot daffs in it.

Cabernet Sauvignon VdP d'Oc Val d'Orbieu, Somerfield

14 B

Superb little number at a superbly little price. Has cherry and plum in rich unison with tannin and acidity.

Chateau Carbonel Cotes du Rhone 1996

15 C

Cherries and plum coat the tongue with a faint earthy tang. Very drinkable style.

Chateau de Caraguilhes, Corbieres 1994

A tough year for this wine and the wine might improve over the next year. But it's decently fruity now with a hint of depth and some smoked plum flavours. A fair enough stab at richness. A solid hitter with food.

Chateau de la Valoussiere, Coteaux du Languedoc, 1995

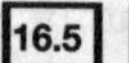 C

Quite superb hairy-chested red of character, richness, food-friendliness, style, earthy herbiness, and rampant individuality. The tannin and fruit are in beautiful liaison.

Chateau Latour Segure Lussac St Emilion 1995

14 D

Very good, warm texture allied to a decent richness of well-toned fruit. Selected stores.

Chateau Le Clairiot Bordeaux 1995

15 C

Chateau Saint Robert, Graves 1993

14 D

Chateau Talence, Premieres Cotes de Bordeaux 1993

12 D

Fades on the finish somewhat, leaving only a dry desert in the throat. Selected stores.

Chateauneuf-du-Pape Domaine de la Solitude, 1995 15 E

Very expensive but divinely delicious.

Claret, Somerfield 14 B

Rather chirpy value for such dry, drinkable, classically styled claret.

Corbieres Val d'Orbieu, Somerfield 12.5 B

Cotes du Rhone Celliers de l'Enclave des Papes 1996, Somerfield 13 B

A light, approachable Rhone of restrained earthiness.

Cotes du Roussillon Jeanjean 13 B

Crozes Hermitage 1995 10 D

Light and dusty.

Fitou Caves de Mont Tauch, Somerfield 14 B

Gigondas Chateau Saint Andre 1995 15.5 D

Delicious – a real quaffing Gigondas of richness and style. Remarkable marinade for the adenoids. Selected stores.

Hautes Cotes de Beaune, Georges Desire 1995 10 D

Made by a man, paradoxically, called Desire.

Medoc NV, Somerfield 14 C

Rich, very determinedly textured and terrific with barbecued meats cooked rare.

Merlot VdP d'Oc Jeanjean 14.5 B

Oak Aged Claret, Somerfield 13 D

Stale cigars on the edge of the fruit.

Saint-Joseph, Cuvee Medaille d'Or, Caves de Saint Desiderat 1991 15 E

St Emilion P. Sichel 13.5 C

Vacqueyras Domaine de la Soleiade 1995 15.5 C

Smells like the inside of a warm gymshoe but the fruit, tannin and acidity are electrifyingly rich and alert. Terrific stuff. Selected stores.

VdP des Cotes de Gascogne Red 1996, Somerfield 11 B

FRENCH WINE WHITE

Ardeche Blanc, Somerfield 11 B

A little limp.

Chablis Premier Cru, Grande Cuvee, La Chablisienne 1990 11 F

Chardonnay VdP d'Oc 1996, Somerfield 14.5 C

Packed with style and quiet, gently flavoursome fruit which is not quirky or over-tropical but finesse-full and very drinkable.

Chardonnay VdP Jardin de la France 1996 14.5 B

Has some decent, demure, melony fruit with compensating acidity. Not a rich wine, but certainly a very drinkable one.

Domaine de Bordeneuve VdP des Cotes de Gascogne Blanc, 1996 15 C

Delightfully fresh-faced youth with acrobatic manners – leaps across the tastebuds with vigour and rich intent.

Domaine de la Tuilerie Chardonnay, Hugh Ryman 1995 15 C

Domaine de Rivoyre Chardonnay VdP d'Oc 1995 15.5 D

Rich, smoky melon fruit with a hint of ripe avocado nicely hanging on to the melon/lemon overtone. An impressively stylish wine for a touch over a fiver. Selected stores.

Entre Deux Mers 1996, Somerfield 13 C

Solid rather than sensational.

Gewurztraminer d'Alsace 1996, Somerfield 14.5 D

Very delicately flavoured, rose-petal perfumed fruit. Delicious aperitif.

Hautes Cotes de Beaune Blanc, Georges Desire 1995 11 D

James Herrick Chardonnay VdP d'Oc 1996 14.5 C

New World restrained by Old World coyness. A chardonnay of subtlety and crisp fruit which is always nicely understated.

Macon Blanc Villages 1995, Somerfield 13 C

Muscadet Sur Lie 1996 12.5 C

Expensive for the style.

Oak Aged Bordeaux Blanc 1995, Somerfield 13.5 C

Not bad – has some dry hints of class. But hints only.

Syrah Rose Val d'Orbieu, VdP d'Oc 1996 13 B

Pretty colour.

VdP des Cotes de Gascogne Blanc 1996, Somerfield 13 B

VdP des Jardins de la France 1996, Somerfield 15 B

Very crisp, flavourful, balanced, finely knitted fruit and acidity, and stylish on the finish. A terrific fish wine.

White Burgundy 1995, Somerfield 12 D

White Burgundy Georges Desire 1995 13.5 C

GERMAN WINE WHITE

Baden Dry NV, Somerfield 10 C

Dullish.

Hock Rudolf Muller, Somerfield 13.5 B

Flowery fruit, off-dry, great on a hot day as a refresher course.

Morio Muskat St Ursula 1995, Somerfield 14 B

Don't sneer at it, wine snobs. Try it when the weather's sultry, just a glass. Its muscat fruit is like drinking grapes (and, curiously, how many wines can you say *that* of?)

Mosel Riesling Halbtrocken, Somerfield 11 B

Niersteiner Spiegelberg Kabinett 1995, Rudolf Muller, Somerfield 14 B

Rheingau Riesling, St Ursula 1995, Somerfield 13 C

Rheinhessen Auslese, Rheinberg Kellerei 1994, Somerfield 13.5 C

HUNGARIAN WINE RED

Bulls Blood, St Ursula 1993 10 B

HUNGARIAN WINE WHITE

Gyongyos Chardonnay 1996 14.5 C

Delicious citric-edged fruit – the perfect fish wine.

ITALIAN WINE RED

Cabernet Sauvignon del Veneto 1996, Somerfield 13.5 C

Nice dry style. Plenty of tannin on those cherries.

Chianti Classico Montecchio 1994 14.5 C

Chianti Classico Rocca della Macie 1990 13.5 E

Chianti Conti Serristori 1996, Somerfield 11 C

Copertino 1994 14 C

Needs food like grass needs a mower – to keep it down. A thoroughly well-flavoured wine.

I Grilli di Villa Thalia, Calatrasi 1993 15.5 C

Deliciously impish red: has character and drinkability, nary a rough edge.

Lazio Rosso 1995, Somerfield 14 B

Earthy, ripe, characterful, a breeze to sip with supper, and well priced. Does need food, though – anything from roast lamb to stuffed aubergines.

Montereale Sicilian Red, Calatrasi 1996 13 B

Soltero Bianco, Settesoli (Sicily) 14 C

A waxy, almost oily Sicilian wine which would be terrific with shellfish and mackerel dishes.

Soltero Rosso, Settesoli (Sicily)

Smells like a sauce you might have with game: rich and pungent. The fruit, at first, seems reluctant, then it opens up in the throat to be soft and plump.

Tuscan Red 1996, Somerfield

Very lightly fruity wine with a hint of earthiness giving it character. Try it chilled.

Valpolicella Fratelli Pasqua 1996, Somerfield

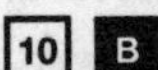

So light you could screw it to a rose in the middle of the ceiling.

Vigneti Casterna Valpolicella Classico, Pasqua 1994

What are the words usually applied to Valpol? The Obscene Publications Act forbids their use in this book. However, with this example such words are unnecessary. It's delicious.

ITALIAN WINE WHITE

Chardonnay del Piemonte Araldica 1996, Somerfield

Rather more expensive than makes for comfortable acquisition but has some suppleness and lemonic-edged butteriness to the fruit.

Le Trulle Chardonnay del Salento 1996 15.5 C

One of the most elegantly fruity, lemonically well-polished and softly melony Italian chardonnays around, at an excellent price.

Montereale Bianco 1996, Somerfield (Sicily) 14.5 B

More nuttiness and flavour than previous vintages. Terrific little fish wine and general, all-purpose, slide-down-any-time tipple.

Orvieto Classico Conti Serristori 1996 13.5 C

A gentle crisp edge to the pear/pineapple fruit is its best feature.

Pinot Grigio Fratelli Pasqua 1996, Somerfield 12 C

Somewhat perfunctory for four quid.

Tuscan White 1996, Somerfield 14.5 B

A rich, creamy, gently nutty wine of some style. A thoroughly commendable glug.

MOLDOVAN WINE WHITE

Kirkwood Moldovan Chardonnay 1996 15 C

Has hints of richness but is never blowsy or overbaked. It's always elegant, purposeful, direct – and hugely drinkable.

NEW ZEALAND WINE — RED

Montana Cabernet Sauvignon Merlot 1995 14.5 D

Grass meets wet earth, but the result, though interesting, is not exactly paydirt. A dry, vegetal wine which needs food.

NEW ZEALAND WINE — WHITE

Coopers Creek Sauvignon Blanc 1996 14 E

Has elegance, undeniably, and it's well crafted – it isn't, though, as racy and individual as previous vintages. Selected stores.

Montana Sauvignon Blanc 1996 14.5 D

Good grassiness smoothly mown and well tended. Loss of impact on the finish but too individual and decently fruity to rate less.

PORTUGUESE WINE — RED

Alta Mesa Tinto Estremadura 1995 15.5 

Brilliant summer quaffing: soft, slightly rich and flavourful and exceedingly friendly.

Dao Reserva, Caves Alianca 1990 14 

Leziria Tinto Almeirim 1995 13.5 B

SOUTH AFRICAN WINE RED

Jacana Pinotage, Stellenbosch 1995 16.5 D

A Devon cream tea, rich and rampant, from the Devon Winery. Has a wonderful savoury aroma, brilliant tannins and fruit, and a persistent finish.

South African Pinotage 1996, Somerfield 13.5 C

SOUTH AFRICAN WINE WHITE

Bellingham Sauvignon Blanc 1996 14.5 C

Why pay for, or drink, sancerre at twice the price? Selected stores.

Jacana Chardonnay, Stellenbosch 1996 15 D

Very rich, ripe, deeply flavoured almost fume fruit of very satisfying drinkability. Great with food.

South African Dry White 1996, Somerfield 14.5 B

An agreeably priced and very agreeably fruited wine: crisp, flavoursome, perky.

SPANISH WINE RED

Berberana Tempranillo, Rioja 1994 15 C

Don Hugo Tinto 1995, Somerfield 13.5 B

Rioja Reserva Vina Cana 1987, Somerfield 14 D

Curiously youthful for such age. Tasty, though, and great with burnt sausages.

Rioja Tinto Almaraz NV, Somerfield 15 C

Gentle coconut and vanilla tone to the fruit. Don't pour it over ice cream – it's better down the throat.

Santara Dry Red Conca de Barbera 1995 14 B

SPANISH WINE WHITE

Almenar Rioja, Somerfield 14 C

Lovely, rich, creamy edge to the crisp frontal attack of the fruit. A terrific all-purpose food wine (salads, soups, poultry, fish, light oriental and Indian food).

Castillo Imperial Blanco 1996 13.5 B

The spritzig edge rather detracts from the overall crispness but with a well-burnt slab of seafood this may not much matter.

Somerfield Valencia Dry White, Vincente Gandia 1996 12 B

Somewhat muted with only an echo of fruitiness as it goes down the gullet.

FORTIFIED WINE

Fino Luis Caballero, Somerfield 15 C

A dry, tea-leaf edged fino of classic bone dryness.

Manzanilla Gonzales Byass, Somerfield 14.5 C

A great opportunity, at this remarkable price, to pit this saline, nutty masterpiece against prawns from the barbecue.

SPARKLING WINE/CHAMPAGNE

Angas Brut Rose (Australia) 15.5 D

Cordoniu Chardonnay Brut 14 D

De Vauzelle Champagne NV 12 F

Not a convincing argument for spending eleven quid.

Mumm Cuvee Napa Brut (California) 13.5 E

Prince William Blanc de Blancs Champagne 13.5 G

Prince William Champagne NV 12 F

Prince William Rose Champagne, Henri Mandois NV 12 G

Seaview Brut 14 D

Seaview Pinot Noir Chardonnay NV 15 E

One of the most elegant Aussie bubblies around. Selected stores.

Somerfield Cava NV 15 D

Somerfield Rose Cava NV 14.5 D

Delicious summer tipple. Selected stores.

Touraine Rose Brut, Caves de Viticulteurs de Vouvray 13 D

Somerfield
Gateway House
Hawkfield Business Park
Whitchurch Lane
Bristol BS14 0TJ
Tel 0117 9359359
Fax 0117 9780629

Summerplonk 1997

TESCO

ARGENTINIAN WINE — WHITE

Picajuan Peak Chardonnay 1996 16 C

Terrific value here. A monstrously-unfair-to-white-burgundy-growers chardonnay of depth, elegance, richness and complexity. The lovely textured fruit makes up for the absence of woody character.

AUSTRALIAN WINE — RED

Australian Cabernet/Merlot, Tesco 13 C

Will probably be coming into store just as this book comes out.

Australian Red, Tesco 14.5 B

It slips down brilliantly like greased damsons and soft fruit (raspberries?). A totally grand glug.

Australian Ruby Cabernet, Tesco 14 C

Australian Shiraz, McLaren Vale 1994, Tesco 15 D

Barramundi Shiraz/Merlot 14 C

Very juicy style with a burnt edge.

Bin 707 Cabernet Sauvignon, Penfolds 1992 18.5 G

Imperious, gargantuan, ravishing. It combines all the elements of excess but makes them deliciously harmonised. One of Australia's most impressive reds. Guts with panache.

Brown Brothers Tarrango 1996 14 C

This rubbery, aromatic, soft, well-flavoured wine is very versatile, meat or fish, and chills uncomplainingly.

Buckley's Clare Valley Cabernet Franc 1994 14 D

Only just rates this much. The juicy fruit is very giving and perky (not a £7 characteristic so much as a £4) but the flavour and food-friendliness win through in the end. But needs food. Selected stores.

Chapel Hill McLaren Vale Cabernet Sauvignon 1993 15 E

Chapel Hill McLaren Vale Shiraz 1995 14 E

Immediately all-embracing of the tastebuds if not so tender on the pocket.

Cockatoo Ridge Cabernet/Merlot 1995 13.5 D

Coonawarra Cabernet Sauvignon 1995, Tesco 15 D

Lovely harmony of fruit, acid and tannin in charming, if somewhat effete and over-elegant, form. But I quibble. 15 points means this is the bee, if not quite its knees.

David Wynn Patriarch Shiraz 1994 14 E

Lovely special picnic treat, this pricey indulgence, with some salami, a warm baguette and butter. Top seventeen stores.

Hardys Nottage Hill Cabernet Sauvignon/ Shiraz 1994 15 

Ironstone Cabernet/Shiraz 1994 15 D

Soft as woolly socks but far more soupy and drinkable. It's very soggy in the middle but this could be said to be mere approachability. But it's deep and flavour-packed. Selected stores.

Kingston Estate Mataro 1994 13 D

Kingston Estate Shiraz 1993 14 D

Kingston Reserve Riverland Shiraz 1992 13 E

Kooralong Sky Red 15 B

Sheer bargain hunter's prize: dry, fruity, balanced, bracingly slurpable and well flavoured.

Leasingham Cabernet Sauvignon/Malbec 1994 15 E

Rich and finely endowed with softness, balance, depth and style. Choose its food, like roast chicken, with care. No spices!! Selected stores.

Leasingham Domaine Shiraz 1994 15.5 D

Wonderful chewy texture and brilliant fruit/acid balance. Has a vivacity and stylishness well worth the money. Quality of fruit and crafted structure – this wine has both.

Lindemans Bin 50 Shiraz 1993 15 

Lindemans Coonawarra Pyrus 1992 15 F

Yes, it's sodden with deliciousness but is it worth £12? Well, whilst food will blunt its superficial richness and depth (so plain food only), I also suspect it's at heart merely a misanthropic sybarite's solo comfort. Top seventeen stores.

Lindemans Limestone Ridge Coonawarra 1992 13 F

Grand glugging at a grand price. Top seventeen stores.

Lindemans St George Cabernet Sauvignon 1992 14 F

A beautifully polished wine of consummate hauteur and class. However, this immaculate demeanour will, I suspect, panic with food of any great flavour (like game, say) while in many respects this is its perfect partner. But it does make delicious quaffing. Top seventeen stores.

Maglieri Shiraz, McLaren Vale 1993 16 D

McLaren Vale Merlot, Rosemount 1993 16 D

Mountadam 'The Red' Cabernet Sauvignon/Merlot 1992 13 F

A terrific £5 glug of depth and style. But a £15 wine? Don't make me laugh. Top seventeen stores.

Old Penola Estate Coonawarra Cabernet Sauvignon 1991 13.5 D

Penfolds Bin 128 Shiraz, Coonawarra 1992 14 E

Penfolds Bin 35 Shiraz Cabernet 1994 15.5 C

Penfolds Kalimna Bin 28 Shiraz 1993 16 E

Rosemount Balmoral Syrah 1993 12 G

Rosemount Estate Shiraz/Cabernet 1996 15.5 C

So soft and slip-downable it may be a crime.

St Halletts Old Block Shiraz 1993 14 E

Stirling Estate Shiraz 1992 15 D

Temple Bruer Cornucopia Grenache 1994 15.5 D

Temple Bruer Shiraz/Malbec 1989 14 D

Thomas Hardy Coonawarra Cabernet Sauvignon 1992 15 F

Lovely texture of softness, dryness, rich deep fruit and wonderful relaxed, giving flavour. Great with game which its excellent fruit/acid/tannic balance can cope with. Top seventeen stores.

Tim Adams Shiraz 1993 14 E

Wynns John Riddoch Cabernet Sauvignon, Coonawarra 1992 13.5 G

Wynns Michael Coonawarra Shiraz 1993 12 H

Ridiculous price for a delicious sippin' wine of fine fruit and rich-edged elegance. But too prissy for rich food and too rich for prissy company. So who gets to enjoy it at £25? Not me. Top seventeen stores.

Yalumba Bushvine Grenache, 1993 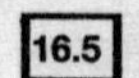 

AUSTRALIAN WINE WHITE

Australian Semillon/Chardonnay 1996, Tesco 13.5 C

Decent rather than daring, respectable instead of rumbustious, oaky rather than ostentatious. Should be coming into store as this book comes out.

Australian White, Tesco 14 B

Good fruit to start, then sags, but then makes it up with a very pleasant lemony finish. Somewhat cool temperamentally for an Aussie.

Best's Colombard 1995 15.5 C

Brown Bros Late Picked Muscat 1995 14.5 D

Interesting sweet aperitif. Rich muscaty fruit, not clammy or too sticky, with an edge of spiced pineapple. Selected stores.

Brown Brothers Riesling 1995 15 D

Hints of powdery lemon sherbet and lime give the fruit charm and some eccentricity. Superb fish wine. Top seventy-seven stores.

Brown Brothers Sauvignon Blanc 1995 14 D

Delicious chewy edge to the ripe fruit gives the wine enhanced food-partnering opportunities. Great with mussel soup. Top seventy-seven stores.

Cape Mentelle Semillon/Sauvignon Blanc 1995 16 E

Chapel Hill Unwooded Chardonnay 1996 13.5 E

Expensive for the level of fruit on offer. It's a good, crisp wine, excellent with seafood, but it costs.

Clare Valley Riesling 1995, Tesco 14.5 C

Hardys Nottage Hill Chardonnay 1996 16 C

Superb soft, rolling texture. Brilliant fruit. Great balance.

Hunter Valley Semillon 1995, Tesco 13.5 D

Interesting, but the finish fails to clinch it for me.

Lindemans Padthaway Chardonnay 1993 15.5 E

Mick Morris Liqueur Muscat (half bottle) 15.5 C

Old Triangle Semillon/Chardonnay 1995 13.5 C

Penfolds Old Vine Semillon 1995 15 D

Ripeness nicely coddled by the woody edge and acidic coating. Delicious structure of class and style. Selected stores.

Penfolds Semillon/Chardonnay 1995 14 D

Pewsey Vale Eden Vale Riesling 1996 15 D

Take your prejudices and throw them to the dogs. This is riesling of measured fruitiness, excellent acid balance, developed flavour and overall very tasty style. It will develop well, and very interestingly, for a couple of years more. Selected stores.

Preece Chardonnay 1994 15 D

Rosemount Estate Chardonnay 1995 16 D

Rosemount Estate Diamond Label Chardonnay 1996 16 D

Rich warm aroma of gently baked fruit, lovely texture with a bias to oiliness and a firm, positive finish. The fruit dominates the finish, over the acidity. A lovely wine, well priced. It has a certain delicacy withal – light poultry and fish dishes only.

Rosemount Estate Sauvignon Blanc 1995 16 D

Rosemount Roxburgh Chardonnay 1994

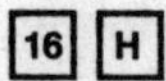

What a price! (£25!) But when you consider the paucity of fruit many meursaults offer at this price, Roxburgh is beautifully calm, poised, deliciously woody and very, very classy. If New World chardonnay must copy Old World chardonnay styles, this is not just a copy – it's fancier than the original.

Shaw & Smith Sauvignon Blanc 1995 13.5 E

Extraordinary cheek! A teenage wine of some charm asking a mature, complex wine price. Has hints of strawberry among the various odd edges to the fruit. Top seventy-seven stores.

Stirling Estate Chardonnay 1995 15 D

Tim Adams Riesling 1995 14.5 E

Gorgeous sherbety texture. Lots of flavour and personality here. Thai food wine par excellence. Top seventy-seven stores.

Tim Adams Semillon 1995 13.5 E

Exotic bouquet, not overblown, just mysterious, leading to fruit which has some texture and finesse. A touch short on the finish for a wine of this price. Selected stores.

AUSTRIAN WINE — RED

Lenz Moser Blauer Zweigelt 1996 

Better priced, better fruited than so many beaujolais with which this fresh, gently elastic-textured young wine bears comparison. I do not mean to insult the Austrian by so saying.

AUSTRIAN WINE — WHITE

Lenz Moser Beerenauslese 1994 (half bottle) 14 D

Lenz Moser Gruner Veltliner 1994 14 C

Lenz Moser Selection Gruner Veltliner 1995 13 C

BRAZILIAN WINE — RED

Brazilian Cabernet Sauvignon/Merlot, Tesco 14 C

BRAZILIAN WINE — WHITE

Brazilian Chardonnay/Semillon, Tesco 14 B

Brazilian Pinot Blanc, Tesco 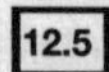 

BULGARIAN WINE RED

Noble Oak Lyaskovets Merlot 1994 

It comes like fruit juice at first gulp – then the richness and gentle tannic undertone appear and give the finish bulk and vigour. A great pasta wine – especially tomato sauced over. Selected stores.

Reka Valley Bulgarian Cabernet Sauvignon, Tesco 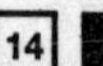 

Not possible to imagine an easier-to-drink cabernet. It just floods down the throat without even wiping its boots on the doormat. A terrific, brilliant-value pasta wine.

BULGARIAN WINE WHITE

Bear Ridge Dry White 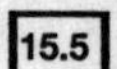 

Brilliant tippling. The fruit is double-layered, edgily rich but nicely counter-pointed by incisive acidity. Terrific value.

CANADIAN WINE RED

Canadian Red, Tesco  

CANADIAN WINE — WHITE

Canadian White, Tesco 13.5 C 

CHILEAN WINE — RED

Carmen Cabernet Sauvignon 1994 14 D

Juicy and ripe yet has a tannic shroud which holds up the flavour and gives it weight and depth.

Chilean Cabernet Sauvignon Reserve 1995, Tesco 16 C 

Rich, rampant, beautifully balanced between mellowness and tannic dryness, and well kitted out with a smooth suit of worsted textured fruit. Classy, lithe, delicious, this is an exhibition of top-class winemaking using first-class grapes.

Chilean Cabernet Sauvignon, Tesco 16 C 

Brilliant fruit here: bold yet soft, fruity yet dry, balanced yet not afraid to stick its neck out. Terrific stuff.

Chilean Red, Tesco 14.5 B

Don Maximo Cabernet Sauvignon 1993 16.5 D

Errazuriz Merlot 1996 17 D 

Totally delicious: textured, dry, multi-layered, gently leathery and enticingly aromatic, rich yet not forbidding, stylish, very classy and overwhelmingly terrific value for money.

Louis Felipe Edwards Reserve Cabernet Sauvignon 1994 17 D

Sheer chutzpah: fruity, rich, chocolatey, consummately drinkable. Fabulous texture of suede and velvet. Top thirty-one stores.

Santa Ines Cabernet/Merlot 1996  

Smooth yet jammy and ripe. Terrific with food. Has well-developed fruit/acid balance. Selected stores.

CHILEAN WINE WHITE

Chilean Chardonnay 1996, Tesco 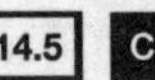

Rich, melony and firmly lemonic on the finish. A grilled fish and shellfish chardonnay.

Chilean Sauvignon Blanc, Tesco  

Superb combination of fresh biting acidity and rich-edged fruit of depth and flavour. It has personality, this wine, though I wish it was still under £3.50.

Chilean White, Tesco  

Errazuriz Chardonnay 1996  

Not as rich and exuberant as many Chilean chardonnays of this year. But it is elegant, decisively balanced, and decently priced for the texture of the fruit and its demurely creamy rich edge.

Errazuriz Chardonnay Reserva 1994 16 D

Santa Ines Sauvignon 1996 14 C

Has the length and hints of opulence which typify Chilean sauvignon. Selected stores.

FRENCH WINE RED

Baron de la Tour Fitou 1995 13.5 C

Interesting baked-earth style – but a touch overpriced.

Beaumes de Venise, Cotes du Rhone Villages 1994 14 D

Bordeaux Rouge 1995 13.5 C

Bourgogne Hautes Cotes de Nuits 12.5 D

Buzet 1991 13.5 C

Cahors, Tesco 12.5 B

Chateau Bessan Segur, Medoc 1995 13 D

Tries very hard.

Chateau Cote Montpezat, Cotes de Castillon 1993 14.5 D

A touch light on the finish but the bouquet and the fruit on the palate are memorable. Dry, stylish, this is a true claret yet one which is very approachable. Selected stores.

Chateau de Goelane Bordeaux 1994 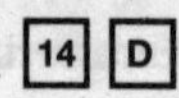

Very well-mannered and polite, this is bordeaux trying to please – and succeeding.

Chateau Lagrave Martillac 1994 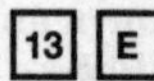

Takes time to invigorate the tongue – due to its youth. But when, after twenty seconds, the finish cruises in after the initial fruity attack, it shows its class. I'd lay it down for another five to eight years. Selected stores.

Chateau Leon Premieres Cotes de Bordeaux 1994  

Real classic claret. Attacks the molars like a horde of Visigoths – loudly, recklessly, dryly and very effectively. Will develop well between now and the millennium.

Chateau Pigoudet, Coteaux d'Aix en Provence 1994 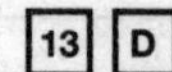

Not as brilliant as previous vintages – seems to lack the richness of yesteryear. Top eighty stores.

Chateau Regusse Coteaux de Pierrevert 1994 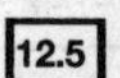 

Vegetal and very fresh. Will it improve over time? It needs to. But it's had three years already. Top thirty stores.

Chateau Robert Cotes de Bourg 1993 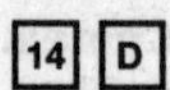

Chateau Saint-Nicholas, Fronsac 1990  D

This is what claret should be like! Classy, dry, tannic, aromatic, deep, uncompromising but beautifully mature and textured, this wine knocks spots off medocs priced four times as much. Perfect drinking now. Really lays into the tastebuds.

Chateau St Georges, St. Emilion 1993 12.5 G

Chateau Trimoulet St Emilion 1989 13 G

Amusing presumptions to class. Hugely overpriced. Top seventy-seven stores.

Chevalier de Gruaud Larose 1992 13 E

Claret, Tesco 14 B

About as inexpensive yet as genuine as claret can possibly get. A bargain.

Corbieres, Tesco 14.5 B

Corbieres shorn of its ragged edges and scrubbed – this is all charm, softness and utter drinkability.

Cotes du Rhone, Tesco 11 B

Couly Dutheuil Chinon, Baronnie Madeleine 1992 16 D

Domaine de Beaufort Minervois 1995, Tesco 12 B

Domaine de Conroy Brouilly, Jean St Charles 1994 11 D

Domaine de Jouclary Carbardes 1993 14 C

Great clods of earth by the bucketful. Top eighty stores.

Domaine de Lanestousse Madiran 1993 14 D

Inviting aroma of dead wood, new shoes and floor cleaner. The fruit is tannin-ravaged, so needs time to settle. But with rare roast beef, today, it would be remarkable company. Otherwise, give it to grandad to soak his teeth in.

Domaine de Pauline Cotes du Rhone 1993 15 C

Domaine de Revest Pinot Noir 1995 10 C

Very light and uninteresting.

Domaine du Soleil Syrah/Malbec 1995 13.5 C

Too expensive when compared with softer, fruitier specimens (especially Chilean). The fruit is brisk, somewhat stern-visaged (but good with rich food) and thus not a congenial glug by itself. Compare with Chateau Caraguilhes which is also organic (but not suitable for vegans as this is).

Domaine du Soleil Vegan Merlot, VdP d'Oc 1994 14 C

Domaine Georges Bertrand Corbieres 1994 16 C

Better than many bordeaux at twice the price, this dry, rich wine has herb-packed denseness of fruit and loads of characterful depth. Excellent fruit, acid and tannins all in meaty collusion. Top thirty stores.

Domaine Maurel Fonsalade, Saint Chinian 1994 14.5 C

Equus Bergerac Rouge 1995 12 C

A dull and bordeaux-like bottle of underdeveloped fruit. It needs eighteen months or so to shake off its torpor and even then I'm not sure we'll have something to set the world, or any palate, on fire. Selected stores.

French Cabernet Sauvignon Reserve, Tesco 14 C

Good jammy fruit held back from overripeness and juiciness by gentle tannins.

French Cabernet Sauvignon, Tesco 

Brilliant value. A beautifully coloured wine of force, character, varietal stylishness and real warm cabernet deliciousness. The peppery, almost cinnamon edge to the wine is balanced by an apple-skin acidity. A fantastic glugging wine and great with all sorts of casseroles, cheese dishes and most vegetables.

French Gamay, Tesco 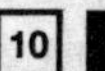 

This could well take the biscuit as the feeblest red on Tesco's shelves. (That's a water biscuit, by the way.)

French Merlot Reserve, Tesco 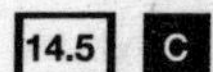 

Immensely drinkable yet with a gamine serious side to its personality. Dark, rich and handsome, this is good value. Hints of classic merlot leatheriness only, but this is *gluggable* merlot.

Great With Steak Merlot d'Oc 1995 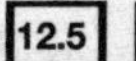 

A disappointment and not great with steak.

Grenache, Tesco 

La Vieille Ferme, Cotes du Rhone 1994 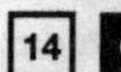

Lacost-Borie, Pauillac 1993

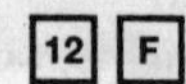

Top seventeen stores.

Le Bahans du Chateau Haut-Brion, Pessac-Leognan 1992

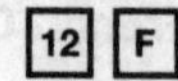

Les Vieux Cepages Carignan VdP de l'Herault

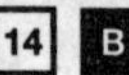

Slightly more nervous of temperament than its grenache brother. But still a bargain.

Les Vieux Cepages Grenache VdP de l'Herault

Love the label! It's as engaging as the dry, herby, earthy wine inside the bottle.

Louis Jadot Beaune Premier Cru 1992

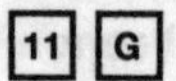

Hint of truffle on the aroma. Not worth three fivers of anyone's dosh, though. Selected stores.

Margaux 1994, Tesco

Real dark fruit with lots of tannic personality. Bristles a bit, needs three years to be at its peak, and it is expensive. Selected stores.

Mas de Daumas Gassac Rouge 1995

Wait another five years. It should rate 16 then. Wine Advisor Stores only.

Minervois, Tesco

A simple, fruity wine which hints at its herby, sun-packed provenance rather than smacking it to you forcibly.

Morgon, Arthur Barolet 1994 11 D

Moulin de la Doline Fitou 1995 14 C

Where is the Peasant Plonk of yesterday? There are tannins here but they're softly integrated with the fruit to provide texture and character.

Moulin de Saint-Francois Corbieres 1993 13.5 D

Mourvedre VdP d'Oc 1995, Tesco 13.5 B

Light and very simple with a good, dry finish.

Nature's Choice Organic Red, Bordeaux Superieur 1994 13 C

Pauillac 1994, Tesco 13 D

Red Burgundy 1995, Tesco 11 C

St Emilion, Tesco 13 D

St Estephe 1993, Tesco 15.5 E

St Joseph Cave de la Tain l'Hermitage 1994 13 D

Top eighty stores.

St Julien 1993, Tesco 15 E

Yvecourt Bordeaux Rouge 1995 13 C

Top eighty stores.

FRENCH WINE WHITE

Alsace Gewurztraminer 1995, Tesco 13.5 D

Expensive but a treat with take-away Peking duck with plum sauce.

Alsace Pinot Blanc, Tesco 11 C

Alsace Riesling Graffenreben 1995 11 D

Anjou Blanc, Tesco 12 B

Bordeaux Sauvignon Blanc 1995 14 C

Cabernet de Saumur Rose, Tesco 13.5 C

A light rose, perfect chilled in large glasses for small back-garden parties (i.e. you and a grilled mackerel on the hot coals).

Chablis 1995, Tesco 13 D

Lot of dosh. Not a lot of posh.

Chardonnay Reserve, Maurel Vedeau 1994 14 C

Chateau Armand Sauternes 1994 (half bottle) 13 E

Rather pricey but good with blue cheese. Top seventy-seven stores.

Chateau de la Colline Bergerac Blanc 1995 15.5 C

Like a fine woody bordeaux blanc. Excellent structure. Top eighty stores only.

Chateau la Foret St Hilaire Entre-Deux-Mers 1995 11 C

Too expensive, insufficiently exciting for a fiver.

Chateau Passavent Anjou Blanc 1994 15.5 C

Chenin Blanc, VdP du Jardin de la France, Tesco 15 B

Brilliant value: impishly fruity (melony yet very crisp and clean to finish), delightfully well paced from aroma to finish, and simply delicious.

Cotes du Rhone Blanc 1996 

Excellent food wine. Has soft, crisp fruit – a paradox peculiar to Rhone whites.

Crozes Hermitage Blanc 1995 11 D

Domaine de la Done Syrah Rose 1996 12.5 B

Selected stores.

Domaine de la Jalousie Late Harvest VdP des Cotes de Gascogne 1993 14 C

Domaine de Montauberon Marsanne 1996 12 C

Doesn't give a lot.

Domaine du Soleil Sauvignon/Chardonnay 1995 (suitable for vegetarians and vegans) 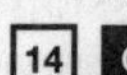

Fresh with a nutty undertone, this wine is perfect with an elegant side of grilled sole. Top eighty stores only.

Domaine Raissac Vermentino/Chardonnay 1996 14.5 B

What a delightful fish wine! It's ready to go with baked cod or even mackerel with mustard sauce. Top eighty stores.

Domaine Saint James Viognier 1995 13.5 D

Pricey for the style which seems a little ill-defined.

Domaines Saint Pierre Chardonnay, Vin de Pays d'Oc 1993 12.5 C

Equus Bergerac Blanc 1995 13 C

Like an ordinary bordeaux blanc. Not a lot of fruit or layers of flavour. Selected stores.

Escoubes, VdP des Cotes de Gascogne, Tesco 14 B

A first-rate welcome-home-from-work glug. Attractive and balanced, fresh and clean.

French Chardonnay, VdP d'Oc, Tesco 12 C

French Vermentino VdP d'Oc 1996 15 B

A superbly fresh, clean, brightly fruity but very well-balanced wine. Excellent with light fish dishes and aperitif situations. Top eighty stores.

Gaston Dorleans Vouvray Demi-Sec 1993 12 C

Great With Chicken Chardonnay d'Oc 1996 12 B

A lie. It would not be great with chicken. It would be adequate.

Great With Fish 1996

Interesting concept. Not a hugely thrilling wine (and it wouldn't necessarily be 'great with fish').

Greenwich Meridian 2000 White, Bordeaux 1996 13.5 C

Pleasant, light, gently floral, crisply edged, romantic with candles. Expensive.

Haut Poitou Sauvignon Blanc 1994 13.5 C

James Herrick Chardonnay 1996 14.5 C

More lemonic than previous vintages and less like the Old World style – but it will, I feel, pull itself round more richly over the next nine months.

James Herrick Chardonnay Reserve 1995 15 D

Has softness and richness and is obviously trying very hard to be high-class chardonnay. It succeeds, but even giving it 15 I wish it was less than seven quid. Top eighty stores.

La Vieille Ferme Cotes du Rhone Blanc 1995 12.5 C

Louis Jadot Pouilly Fuisse 1994 12 F

Macon Blanc Villages 1996, Tesco 13.5 C

Not bad, not bad at all. But is it a fiver's worth of fruit? Not compared with Chile or South Africa.

Mas de Daumas Gassac White 1996 10 F

Almost sweet in its kindergarten fruitiness. Astonishing presumption to charge eleven quid for such wine – even if the red is one of the best reds in southern France. Curious! Wine Advisor Stores only.

Meursault Louis Josse 1994 11 G

You really have to search for Monsieur Josse's name on the label. I'm not surprised he's trying to make himself as inconspicuous as possible.

Muscat Cuvee Jose Sala 1996 

As good, sweetly dispositioned, honeyed, waxy and good value as ever. Lovely with pud.

Muscat de Beaumes de Venises (half bottle) 

Muscat de Rivesaltes (half bottle) 

Brilliant solo-hedonist's summer Saturday afternoon treat on the patio: good book, this little half bottle, a baguette, some Italian blue cheese and a big bunch of red grapes.

Oak Aged White Burgundy 1995, Tesco 

Organic White, Tesco 

Roussanne VdP d'Oc 1996, Tesco 

Slightly peachy edge to the fruit makes it very agreeable – even if, at £3.99, it seems a touch on the high side.

Russian Oak Reserve Chenin/Chardonnay  

Only the wood the barrels are made from comes from Russia. The grapes come from the Languedoc. I feel the relationship between the two is not as mellow and harmonious as the price would suggest. Top thirty stores.

Sancerre 1995, Tesco 10 D

Dull, mean, overpriced. Tesco must stock sancerre, customers demand it, but why are these customers so ignorant of better Tesco whites at half the price? Answer: sancerre has a name.

Saubagnere Sauvignon/Colombard, VdP de Gascogne 1995

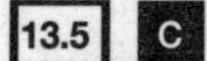

Young and frisky. Has hints of opulence.

Sauvignon Blanc Bordeaux, Tesco

Good food tipple. Has a characteristic hint of earthiness to its fruit. Crisp finish. decent value.

Sauvignon Blanc Selection Jean-Marie Johnston, VdP d'Oc 1995

Sauvignon de St Bris 1995

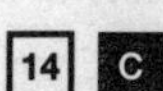

Semillon Bordeaux, Tesco

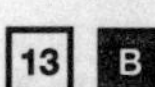

St Veran Les Monts 1995

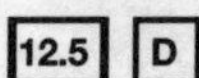

Expensive but not bad as white burgundies go. But I'm trying really hard to like it. Top eighty stores.

Viognier Les Domaines Viennet 1996, Tesco

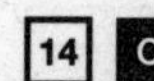

Gentle apricot edge, fresh urgent acidity – a very pleasant palate-tickling tipple. Should be coming into selected stores as this book comes out.

White Graves, Tesco

GERMAN WINE — RED

Echo Hill Baden Pinot Noir 1993 13 

GERMAN WINE — WHITE

Bernkasteler Kurfurstlay, Tesco 13 B

German Pinot Blanc, Tesco 12 C

Mosel Kabinett, Tesco 11 B

Nahe Kabinett, Tesco 12 B

Some hints of bulk to the fruit and zip to the acidity.

Palatinarum Riesling, Zimmerman Graeff 1995 12.5 C

Rather expensive for the simplicity of the lemony fruit. Nice with grilled prawns, though.

Palatinarum Rivaner, Zimmerman Graeff 1995 13 C

Pfalz Kabinett, Tesco 11.5 B

Selected stores.

Scharles Kerner Kabinett Halbtrocken 1995 (50 cl) 12 C

Steinweiler Kloster Liebfrauenberg Auslese, Tesco 13 D

Rich, gently honeyed, sweet to finish. Decent enough tipple with fresh fruit.

Steinweiler Kloster Liebfrauenberg Kabinett, Tesco 13.5 C

Acidity saves it from overweening sweetness. Wouldn't say no to a glass on a hot afternoon.

Steinweiler Kloster Liebfrauenberg Spatlese, Tesco 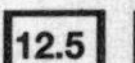 C

Falls off at the end. Rather liked it till then.

GREEK WINE — RED

Nemea 1992 13.5 C

HUNGARIAN WINE — RED

Reka Valley Hungarian Merlot, Tesco  B

Merlot in its juicy foot-bath mode. Soften those bunions up a treat.

HUNGARIAN WINE WHITE

Chapel Hill Hungarian Irsai Oliver 1994 13.5 B

Hungarian Oak Aged Chardonnay, Tesco 13 C

Hmm . . .

Oaked Chardonnay, Szekszard 1995 13.5 B

Reka Valley Hungarian Chardonnay, Tesco 12 B

Vegetal and needs food.

ITALIAN WINE RED

Barolo Giacossa Fratelli 1991 14 D

Worth looking out for the odd bottle that might be left on the shelves, but the '92 should just be coming into store as this book comes out (not available for tasting at time of going to press).

Cabernet Sauvignon del Veneto, Tesco 13.5 B

Cantina del Taburno 1994 13.5 C

Carignano del Sulcis 1994 (Sardinia) 16 C

All tobacco, all-spice and a hint of chocolate. Dry, warm, very sunny of disposition, a touch of exoticism on the finish, and a lingering finish of dry figs and bitter chocolate with an almond edge. Complex enough for you? It was for me.

Chianti Classico Riserva 1991, Tesco 14 D

Chianti Rufina 1995, Tesco 13.5 C

Fresh and young.

Great With Pasta Montepulciano d'Abruzzo 1995 12 B

Light and cherryish and dry – but not a convincing pasta wine.

Marchese del Casa Sicilian Red, Tesco 10 B

Merlot del Piave, Tesco 14 B

A delicate merlot of such coy disposition a sworn white wine lover would find it agreeable. This is not a criticism. It is a positive feature of a dry but demurely fruity red wine.

Merlot del Trentino, Tesco 14 C

Monica di Sardegna, Tesco 11 B

Petit Verdot Casale del Giglio 1995 14 C

Good balance of tannin and acid, fruit a touch begging. But brilliant with food – anything from courgette souffle to leg of lamb. Selected stores.

Pinot Noir del Veneto, Tesco 12 B

Rosso di Montalcino 1993, Tesco 13.5 D

Shiraz Casale del Giglio 1995 14 C

Not like Aussie shiraz, this has more acidity and so is better with Italian food. The wine will develop interestingly in bottle for two more years. It will rate more in six months, I shouldn't wonder.

Sorbaiano Rosse delle Miniere Montescudaio Rosso 1993 16 E

Valpolicella Amarone 1990 12 D

Villa Pigna Cabernasco 1994 16.5 D

A most individual and wickedly drinkable wine. It has rich fruitiness with a herby and burnt – almost charcoal – edge and there is solid accompaniment from tannin and acid. The savouriness of the fruit on the finish is a marvel to behold. Great with a roast dinner.

Vila Pigna Rosso Piceno 1992 16 B

A deliciously well-intentioned wine with plum/cherry fruit which has an edge of marzipan dryness. Far from heavy, it's rich yet very gluggable with a good fresh undertone of acidity and tannins. Excellent balance, stylish in all departments, this is thorough-going good value.

ITALIAN WINE WHITE

Bianco di Custoza, Barbi 1995 13.5 C

Catarratto di Sicilia, Tesco 13.5 C

Chardonnay del Veneto, Tesco 13 B

Frascati 1996, Tesco 13 C

Respectable rather than exciting – and a touch pricey.

Greco di Puglia 1995, Tesco 13.5 C

Nuragus di Cagliari, Tesco 12 B

Pinot Grigio del Veneto, Tesco 14 B

Prosecco del Veneto, Tesco 13.5 B

Salice del Salentino Bianco 1995 12.5 C

Sauvignon Blanc del Veneto, Tesco 12.5 B

Sicilian White, Tesco 14 B

Soave Classico 1995, Tesco 13.5 C

Expensive but rather interesting. It would be delicious with Thai prawns or squid.

Stowells of Chelsea Chardonnay Trentino (3-litre box) 13.5 G

Taburno Falanghina 1994 11 D

Trulle Chardonnay del Salento 1995 15 C

This is a controlled, gorgeously fluent wine of style, complexity and thirst-quenching crispness yet fruitiness. Not at all stores.

Vermentino di Sardegna 15 B

Has a delicious multi-layered, gently citric fruitiness of utter charm.

Villa Cerro Recioto di Soave 1993 (50 cl) 15 C

Off-dry and quirky, this is a delicious hedonistic treat for the solo tippler in the half-litre bottle. Gently waxy and glucoid, its richness has acidity packed in behind so it's never cloying. Might be worth trying with goat's cheese and fresh fruit. Top eighty stores.

Villa Pigna Chiara 13 B

Good with fish and chips; rather meagre without.

MEXICAN WINE RED

L A Cetto Petite Syrah 1993 16 C

Great flourish of fruity depth as the wine disappears down the throat.

MOROCCAN WINE RED

Moroccan Red 14 B

NEW ZEALAND WINE RED

Coopers Creek Merlot 1994 15.5 D

New Zealand Cabernet Sauvignon, Tesco 14 C

New Zealand Cabernet Sauvignon/Merlot 1992, Tesco 13 C

NEW ZEALAND WINE WHITE

Brancott Estate Sauvignon Blanc 1994 12.5 F

Cooks Chardonnay 1996 13.5 C

Respectable, very respectable.

Coopers Creek Chardonnay, Gisborne 1995 15.5 E

Complexity, flavour, style, individuality, admittedly a high price but real class in evidence and overall thoroughly delicious.

Jackson Estate Sauvignon Blanc 1996 16 E

Why buy Tesco's sancerre when for a quid more you can get the real sauvignon taste here? Elegant minerality here, which used to be sancerre's trademark. Now it's Marlborough's. Top thirty stores.

Montana Sauvignon Blanc 1996 14.5 D

Good grassiness smoothly mown and well tended. Loss of impact on the finish but too individual and decently fruity to rate less.

New Zealand Dry White, Tesco 13.5 C

New Zealand Sauvignon Blanc 1995, Tesco 14 C

Stoneleigh Marlborough Chardonnay 1995 14 D

Touch pricey but has genuine hint of its pedigree (Marlborough), even if this is a little muted.

Villa Maria Chenin/Chardonnay 1994 14.5 C

Villa Maria Sauvignon Blanc 1994 (half bottle) 14 B

PERUVIAN WINE RED

Peru Red, Tesco 13 C

Fruity and drinkable, but for a quid less Hungary, Bulgaria and Romania knock it into a cocked hat. If it helps you to swallow £3.99 for this wine, please feel free to drink it out of said headgear. Selected stores.

PERUVIAN WINE WHITE

Peru White, Tesco 13.5 C

Almost excellent. Rich fruit, classily intentioned, but I wish it wasn't so close to £4. Selected stores.

PORTUGUESE WINE RED

Borba Alentejo 1995 

Fabulous value, rich fruit and terrific food-compatibility. A wine to celebrate life with (glass after glass).

Campo Dos Frades Cabernet Sauvignon 1995 15 C

Smoky, rich, tobacco-scented, deep, dry, full of flavour and very gripping. Excellent value. Selected stores.

Dao 1992, Tesco 12 B

Dom Jose, Tesco 12.5 B

Douro 1992, Tesco 12 C

Garrafeira Fonseca 1984 12 C

JP Barrel Selection 1991 17 C

Possibly the best red wine bargain on Tesco's shelves, this roaring broth of a wine. Aromatic, mature, tarry, figgy without being over-ripe, this is a seriously hairy-chested wine of richness, depth, warmth, texture and superb fruit/acid balance with attendant tannins bringing up the rear. Brilliant with casseroled veg and meats. Top eighty stores.

PORTUGUESE WINE WHITE

Dry Vinho Verde, Tesco 13 B

ROMANIAN WINE RED

Romanian Cellars Pinot Noir/Merlot 16 

SOUTH AFRICAN WINE RED

Beyers Truter Pinotage 1995, Tesco 15 C

In a French wine, the dryness hits you immediately, then the fruit. In a South African wine, it's all fruit at first, then the dryness reaches across and hits the palate. Different folks, different strokes.

Clearsprings Cape Red (3-litre box) 14 E

Clos Malverne Auret 1995 14 E

Expensive, dry, delicious – an unusual treat with its rich fruit and dry incisiveness. Top thirty stores.

Diermersdal Merlot 1996 14 D

Has great initial richness then marks time before it deigns to finish. Top eighty stores.

Diermersdal Syrah 1996 13.5 D

Good fruit but somewhat overpriced at nearly six quid. Top eighty stores.

Fairview Merlot 1995 16.5 D

Aggressive, gentle, soft, hard, rich, shallow – this is a bucketful of oxymoronic fruit. It's tannic and very full-bodied but equally elegant and very, very classy. A rustic in rich, royal dress.

Fairview Shiraz 1995 16.5 D

Gorgeous texture where the integrated fruit, tannin and acidity move purposefully and richly over the tongue like a battalion of leather-clad, blackcurrant-dyed centurions determined to fight fair.

International Winemaker Cabernet Sauvignon/Merlot,Tesco 13 C

Charcoal edge to the fruit.

Jennsberg Cabernet Sauvignon/Merlot 1995 13.5 C

Has some aromatic conviction but lets go a little on the finish. Top eighty stores.

Leopard Creek Cabernet/ Merlot 16 C

Great blend of grapes providing the dry, peppery cabernet with the textured, aromatic richness of merlot. Terrific price for the style.

Oak Village Pinotage/Merlot 1996 16 C

Brilliant marriage of the vivacious pinotage and the cerebral merlot.

Oak Village Vintage Reserve, Stellenbosch 1995 14 C

Warm, inviting, with a lovely dryness to the edge of the fruit which lingers. Good texture, balance and style.

Paarl Cabernet Sauvignon, Tesco 15 C

Cabernet in its most approachable, warmly fruity, gluggable style.

Plaisir de Merle Cabernet Sauvignon 1994 12.5 E

Fruity, boot-leather aroma and good fruit but it's a lot of money and fails to convince on the finish. It's not complex as it goes down and thus fails to linger. Selected stores.

Schoone Gevel Merlot 1995 14 C

Hints at juiciness but holds back. Good texture and finish.

South African Red, Tesco 15 B

Lovely glugging here with touches of tar and raspberry. Great chilled with a fish stew. Brilliant at room temperature with casseroles.

South African Reserve Cabernet Sauvignon 1996, Tesco 15 C

Wonderful richness and flavour: dry, characterful, richly styled yet controlled. Good with food.

South African Reserve Shiraz 1995, Tesco  

Has a delightfully savoury and inviting aroma, brisk, serious, rich fruit with tannic edge of dry distinction, and a herby finish of some panache. A terrific wine – even at seven quid. Top eighty stores, from July 1997.

South African Shiraz/Cabernet Sauvignon 1995, Tesco 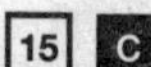

Juicy, deep, very sizzlingly conceived.

Stellenbosch Merlot, Tesco 15 C

Handsome fruit with terrific texture. Has warmth, flavour and richness. Great with meat and vegetable dishes, and cheeses.

Swartland Cabernet Sauvignon/Shiraz 1996 

Rich and hints at cragginess but it softens. without yielding its dark depths, on the finish and pulls off successfully a solid structure. Selected stores.

Vredendal Maskam 1995 15.5 C

Has a lovely juicy depth which manages to avoid jamminess by virtue of some tannic dryness, subtle but firm. Attractive fruit all round. This is first-class tippling.

SOUTH AFRICAN WINE WHITE

Cape Bay Semillon/Chardonnay 15 B

Rich, nutty, floral hints, rich edge, typical exotic feel to the wine – especially the finish.

Cape Chenin Blanc, Tesco 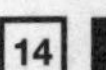 

Freshness, flavour and style – the customary pear-drop flavoured fruit. Hints of ripeness but it isn't overdone. A really welcoming glug.

Cape Colombard/Chardonnay, Tesco 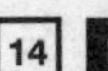

Oodles of flavour, good balance but the fruit forward, good with food.

Danie de Wet Chardonnay Green Label 1996  

On the citric side of fruity but this fruit knows its place and keeps pace with the acidity – which has mineral hints. Has restraint and elegance.

Fairview Sauvignon Blanc/Chenin Blanc 1996 15.5 C

Superb example of first-class white wine at a low price. The wine is whistle-clean but also impishly fruity, well balanced, firm of texture, and resists flirtation with the palate in favour of a serious, deep relationship.

Franschoek Semillon, Tesco 14 C

Has a subtle crispness under the melony fruitiness which is engaging and good with salads and starters.

Goiya Kgeisje 1996 14 C

Very clean and fresh. Great shellfish wine.

La Motte Sauvignon Blanc 1996 15 D

Gives sancerre drinkers, paying £3 more a bottle, food for thought. Top eighty stores.

Leopard Creek Chardonnay 1995 15 C

Richness, style, depth, flavour, balance.

Long Mountain Dry Riesling 1996 13 C

This is unbelievably lean in the fruit department. If a Chilean chardonnay is oak, this is a bamboo reed. It isn't a bad wine, merely raw and very young. It will develop manners over eighteen months to three years but it will never become fruitier. Seafood is its partner – fresh, raw, saline.

Oak Village Chenin/Chardonnay 1996 13 C

Oak Village Sauvignon Blanc 1996 13.5 C

Nutty, fresh, thoroughly decent.

Overgaauw Chardonnay 1996

Quietly stylish, subtly rich, coolly classy. A wine of thought-provoking qualities.

Rylands Grove Barrel Fermented Chenin Blanc 1996

Delicious crispness and tonal fruitiness. The style is nutty and lemonic, but there is a richer, waxier shading in the background. Perfect with any type of seafood – but especially crab cakes.

Rylands Grove Chenin/Colombard 1996

Lovely pebbly textured fruit with melon/mango/lime characteristics. Fresh and flavourful without being blowsy or too amorously young and raw. Selected stores.

Rylands Grove Sauvignon Blanc 1996

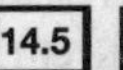

Has that lovely sunny edge to the clean fruit which hints at gooseberry rather than shouting it. A good classically styled sauvignon. Selected stores.

South African Chardonnay/Colombard, Tesco

Exuberant fruit with rich, incisive acidity making a first-class double act of richness with gluggability.

South African Reserve Chardonnay 1996, Tesco

The most elegant and harmonious of Tesco's SA chardonnays. Beautiful wood and fruit integration. Very classy, well-textured.

Swartland Sauvignon Blanc 1996, Tesco 13 C

Somewhat expensive for the style.

Van Loveren Blanc de Noirs Muscadelle 1996 15 B

One of the most delicious examples of the deservedly despised rose genre: lovely rich, dark cherry edge. Selected stores.

Van Loveren Special Late Harvest Gewurztraminer 1996 (half bottle) 14 C

Light and gently honeyed, more of an aperitif than a dessert wine. Personally, I'd lay it down for three to four years to really develop complexity in bottle.

Vergelegen Sauvignon Blanc 1996 14.5 D

Has freshness and flavour – not as common as you might think with sauvignon blanc.

SPANISH WINE RED

Agramont Garnacha 1995 14.5 C

Don Darias 14 B

Marques de Chive Tempranillo 13.5 B

Marques de Grinon Rioja 1994 15.5 C

Marques de Chive Reserva 1989, Tesco 16.5 C

The aroma, of poached egg and wood, is quirky, but the

blackcurrant and plum fruit sears the throat deliciously and the hints of wild strawberry and dried fig will accompany spicy lamb dishes a treat.

Marques de Grinon Syrah 1993 17.5 E

Rioja Vina Mara, Tesco 13.5 C

Torres Coronas 1992 13 C

Torres Sangredetoro 1994 16 C

Brilliant! Best vintage yet!

Vina Mara Rioja Alavesa 16 C

Vina Mara Rioja Reserva 1990, Tesco 13.5 C

Mild-mannered and quiet.

Vina Mayor Ribero del Duero 1991 14.5 C

SPANISH WINE WHITE

Agramont Navarra Viura Chardonnay 1995 15 C

Castillo de Monjardin Chardonnay 1995 14.5 C

The '95 vintage of this wine is somewhat muted at the moment. Little presence aromatically, fruit on the acidic side rather than mellow – but it will improve over a year in bottle. Selected stores.

Vina Mara Superior Rioja, Tesco  

URUGUAYAN WINE — RED

Pacific Peak Tannat/Merlot 1996, Tesco 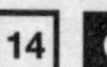 C

Interesting gawkiness but will knit together and develop well over the next six months (I tasted it in September 1996). The wine will go well with food.

URUGUAYAN WINE — WHITE

Pacific Peak Chardonnay/Sauvignon 1996, Tesco  

Has a curious effect of imagining it is a blend of Cape chardonnay and Loire sauvignon. Such is the Uruguayan style profile. An interesting, well-fruited wine of classy hints.

USA WINE — RED

Californian Zinfandel, Tesco 14 C

E & J Gallo Turning Leaf Cabernet Sauvignon 1994 13.5 

Gallo Sonoma County Cabernet Sauvignon 1992 

E

USA WINE — WHITE

August Sebastiani's White Zinfandel 1994 12.5 C

E & J Gallo Turning Leaf Chardonnay 1994 14 D

Gallo Sonoma Chardonnay 1993 17 E

Weston Estate Californian Chardonnay 1995 16.5 D

Weston Super Fruit! Brilliant rich fruit, woody edge, terrific balancing acidity and overall great length and richness. Super value. Selected stores.

FORTIFIED WINE

10 Year Old Tawny Port 13 E

Australian Aged Tawny Liqueur Wine, Tesco 14.5 E

Finest Madeira, Tesco 14 D

Special Reserve Port, Tesco 14 D

Tesco Tawny Port 13.5 D

SPARKLING WINE/CHAMPAGNE

Asti Spumante, Tesco 13 C

Blanc de Blancs Champagne, Tesco 13 G

Blanc de Noirs Champagne, Tesco 13.5 E

Cava, Tesco 16 C

Why drink anything else less well rated in the bubbly department when this gently fruity, elegant fizz is still under a fiver?

Champagne Nicolas Feuilate Brut Premier Cru 15 G

Champagne Premier Cru Brut, Tesco 13.5 E

Chapel Hill Sparkling Chardonnay (Hungary) 14.5 C

Crisp, dry, properly fruity (i.e. restrained rather than full). Excellent value, better than dozens of champagnes penny for penny.

Chardonnay Spumante 13.5 D

Cremant de Bourgogne 1991, Tesco 12 D

Appley and adolescent and advanced in price. Top eighty stores.

Deutz (New Zealand) 15.5 E

Freixenet Brut Rose (Spain) 14.5 D

Jansz Tasmanian Sparkling 12 E

La Marca Prosecco Spumante (Italy) 14 D

Lindauer Brut 13.5 D

Louis Massing Grand Cru Blanc de Blancs 13.5 F

One of those lemony champagnes which I ache to stick creme de cassis or some such adulterant into to give it some oomph . . .

Millennium Champagne, Tesco 13 G

The wittiest thing about it is the price: £19.99. I have to confess, however, to preferring bubbly with dark age price tags: £4.99. Selected stores.

Robertson South African Sparkling, Tesco 13 D

Fruity – not very elegant.

Rose Cava, Tesco 14.5 C

Simonsig Kaapse Vonkel 1992 (South Africa) 13 E

Has an individuality of flavour and style. Top eighty stores.

South African Sparkling Sauvignon Blanc 1996 (Tesco) 13.5 C

Very fruity bubbly. But not sweet. Just very fruity. Hasn't the finesse of Cava at the same price.

Sparkling Chardonnay 1992, Tesco (Australia) 13 D

Sparkling Chardonnay, Tesco (France) 

Vintage Cava 1992, Tesco 16 D

Touch creamier and more opulent than the Tesco non-vintage Cava, but then, justifiably, it's two quid more.

Tesco
Tesco House
PO Box 18
Delamare Road
Cheshunt EN8 9SL
Tel 01992 632222
Fax 01992 644235

WAITROSE

ARGENTINIAN WINE RED

La Bamba Mendoza Pinot Noir/Syrah 1996 14 C

What excellent company to have with a pizza lunch in the back garden. It's rich and soft, sinewy and athletic – it leaps pesto, tomato, American hot and even tuna with ease.

La Bamba Mendoza Tempranillo 1996 15 C

ARGENTINIAN WINE WHITE

Bodega Lurton Pinot Gris, Mendoza 1996 12 C

Santa Julia Torrontes, Mendoza 1996 14 C

AUSTRALIAN WINE RED

Australian Malbec/Ruby Cabernet 1996, Waitrose 14 C

Very jammy and ripe but great with pasta dishes.

Brown Brothers Tarrango 1996 14 C

Browns of Padthaway Cabernet Malbec 1995 13 E

Bottled sunshine, boot polish and plums.

Bushman's Crossing Dry Red 12.5 C

Not been in the saddle long enough – it's light, cherryish, rather feeble with food.

De Bortoli Windy Peak Pinot Noir, Victoria 1996 13 E

Good gamy pinot nose – touch of wild strawberry. Light thereafter, though very drinkable (but eight quid is eight quid).

Hardys Southern Creek Shiraz/Cabernet, SE Australia 1996 13.5 C

Ho-hum finish to a decent level of fruit up-front succeeds in giving it a lower rating.

Orlando Jacob's Creek Shiraz/Cabernet 1995 13.5 C

Reliable if not exciting. Getting pricey this close to a fiver.

Oxford Landing Cabernet/Shiraz 1995 13 C

Penfolds Bin 2 Shiraz/Mourvedre 1995 15.5 D

Rich, dry, stylish, this has fluidity of fruit yet tannic firmness of tone.

Penfolds Rawson's Retreat Bin 35 Cabernet/Shiraz 1994 15.5 C

Ridgewood Mataro Grenache, SE Australia 1996 13 C

Light, pleasant, non-fussy, rather bashful.

Tatachilla Cabernet Sauvignon 1995 14 E

Soft, very soft and very likeable. It ought to rate more at this price but it is only modestly complex and demanding.

Tatachilla Merlot 1995 14 E

Only just makes 14 at this price. It's deep and rich and well-textured upfront but it is uncertain at the finish.

Windy Peak Pinot Noir, Victoria 1996 12 E

Silly price for such uneventful tippling.

Yaldara Old Vine Grenache, Barossa Valley 1996 15 D

Lovely ripe fruit with soft, rich, persistent tannins. Unusually well-organised wine from Oz at this price. It makes fewer concessions to likeability and concentrates on being characterful.

Yaldara Reserve Grenache, Whitmore Old Vineyard 1996 14.5 D

Vivacious, dry, textured, plummy yet full of fleshy fruit which finishes impressively.

AUSTRALIAN WINE WHITE

Australian Riesling/Gewurztraminer 1996, Waitrose

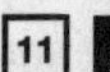

Brown Brothers Late Harvest Riesling 1995 (half bottle) 14 C

Honey and elderflowers – a real treat to drink with fresh fruit. Or cellar it for five years and open nectar.

Bushman's Crossing, SE Australia 1996 13.5 B

Not bad for fish 'n' chips.

Cape Mentelle Semillon/Sauvignon 1996 14.5 E

Gently grassy and melony with a nuttiness lurking on the finish. Stylish but expensive.

De Bortoli Rare Dry Botrytis Semillon, SE Australia 1993 12 E

Hardys Nottage Hill Chardonnay 1995 15.5 C

Hardys Southern Creek Semillon/Chardonnay 1996 13.5 C

Has some flavour.

Lindemans Bin 65 Chardonnay 1996 15.5 C

Delicious combination of butter, hazelnuts and melon undercut by a perfectly weighted uptide of acidity.

Penfolds Barrel Fermented Semillon 1994 14 D

I must confess that it's quirky but brash. The fruit is chewy and rich and perhaps more than a glass or two is difficult to take, but with food (fish or poultry) it's in its element. It can even cope with a mezze.

Penfolds Bin 202 South Australian Riesling 1996 14.5 C

It's the texture which gives it its class. The fruit is lemony and smoky melony, excellent for oriental food, and it would also serve barbecues splendidly.

Penfolds Clare Valley Organic Chardonnay/ Sauvignon Blanc, 1996 14 E

One of the classiest organic whites around: thick fruit of richness and flavour.

Penfolds Koonunga Hill Chardonnay 1996 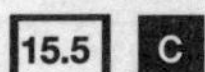

Best vintage for years: aromatic, rich, balanced, food-friendly.

Rosemount Show Reserve Chardonnay 1995 16 E

One of Australia's most incisively fruity chardonnays, with huge hints of class, depth, balance and persistence. Expensive but very fine.

Saltram Mamre Brook Chardonnay 1995 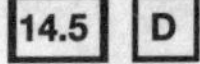

Tatachilla Sauvignon/Semillon 1996 13.5 D

Has some flavour but lacks excitement.

CHILEAN WINE RED

Concha y Toro Merlot 1996  C

So drinkable – it slides down like an eel on skates. So it's smooth but is it fruity? Yes, it's like pureed leather.

Cono Sur Cabernet Sauvignon 1995 15.5 C

Forget the cabernet grape – this is an extra-terrestrial grape of richness, ineffable velvety texture and tremendous length of flavour. Lovely wine.

Isla Negra Cabernet Sauvignon 1996 15.5 C

A wonderfully well fleshed out cabernet of rich texture, soft murky depths and true style. Individual and very drinkable.

Las Cumbres Chilean Dry Red 1995 15 B

Stowells of Chelsea Chilean Merlot Cabernet (3-litre box) 10 G

CHILEAN WINE WHITE

Isla Negra Chardonnay 1996 14 C

Classy stuff – great fish wine.

San Andres Chardonnay, Lontue 1996 14 C

Flavour and style in biting collusion.

San Andres Sauvignon Blanc, Lontue 1996 15 B

Superb roundness of flavoured fruit which finishes briskly. Great price.

Stowells of Chelsea Chilean Sauvignon Blanc (3-litre box) 15.5 F

Valdivieso Chardonnay 1996 16.5 C

Ah! What sublime fruitiness, almost as creamy-rich as a rice pud! This unorthodox assault is, however, controlled, if passionate and very, very delicious. Hugely impressive.

ENGLISH WINE RED

Chapel Down Epoch I East Sussex 1995 14.5 C

Well, well, it's not only drinkable but one in the eye for sceptics like me who regard English red wine as an idea as daft as Japanese clog dancers. It's soft, very handsomely fruity and not obscenely priced. It's as good as any German dornfelder any day.

ENGLISH WINE WHITE

Chiltern Valley Medium Dry 1993 14 C

Individual, ripe, smoky, quaint, balanced, richly flavoured, ignore the 'medium' tag and drink for the pleasure of it – or pair it with fish.

Tanners Brook 7 B

FRENCH WINE RED

Beaujolais 1995, Waitrose 12 C

Bergerac Rouge 1995

Cahors Cotes d'Olt Cuvee Reserve 1994

Needs a year or more to show its real face.

Chateau Croix St Benoit, St Estephe 1994

Chateau des Combes Canon, Canon-Fronsac 1995

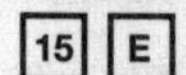

It's the texture and the allied flavour which meld so beautifully and make the wine worth the money. A really classy claret here.

Chateau Haut d'Allard Cotes de Bourg 1995

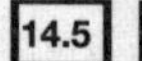

Brilliant barbecued lamb chop wine: rich, dry, meaty, well-balanced. Real flavour here for a penny change out of a fiver.

Chateau La Brunette Bordeaux 1995

Brisk, business-like, a touch formulaic but a good price for the richness of the final finish.

Chateau La Pointe, Pomerol 1993

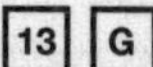

Impressive – but mostly because one admires the sheer cheek of the price tag. For nigh on £18 I'd like the earth to move – not be in my mouth.

Chateau Malescasse, Haut-Medoc 1994

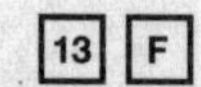

Yes. It's assuredly classy. But I'd be inclined to drink it in three to four years to justify that price.

Chateau Segonzac Premieres Cotes de Blaye, 1994 14.5 D

Chateau Senejac, Haut-Medoc 1993 13.5 E

Almost terrific . . . but over eight quid? Well . . . (pause for thought) . . .

Chateau Villepreux Bordeaux Superieur 1995 15.5 C

Well-priced, well-fruited claret of exceedingly developed tannins and lithe muscularity of fruit. A very handsome bottle for the money.

Clos Saint Michel Chateauneuf-du-Pape 1995 13.5 E

Delicious but expensive. Not, perhaps, as 'big' a wine as previous examples of this vineyard.

Cotes de Ventoux 1995 15 B

Cotes du Rhone 1995, Waitrose 14 C

One of the smoothest and most softly textured Rhone reds around at this price.

Crozes-Hermitage Cave des Clairmonts 1994 13.5 D

There might still be a few bottles of this vintage on the shelves, but the '95 should be coming into store as the book comes out (not tasted at time of going to press).

Domaine de Rose Merlot/Syrah, VdP d'Oc 1996 14 B

Perfect back-garden labelling. Perfect back-garden, cherry-edged, dry fruit in the bottle. Will chill well, too. Serve with any fish or meat from the barbecue.

Domaine de Serame Syrah VdP d'Oc 1996 14.5 C

Perfect summer wine, chilled or warm. Its fruit is already warm, smooth and ripe and it's sinfully easy to glug.

Domaine des Fontaines Merlot, Vin de Pays d'Oc 1995 15 B

Domaine Fontaine de Cathala Syrah/ Cabernet Cuvee Prestige VdP d'Oc 1994 (half bottle) 15 A

Domaine Sainte Lucie Gigondas 1994 17 D

This continues to improve brilliantly in bottle. Superb balance of fruit, acidity and tannins. The lingering berry richness accomplishes what many a Chateauneuf fails to do at twice the price. Great value under seven quid. A massively chewy wine of huge savoury depth and style.

Good Ordinary Claret Bordeaux, Waitrose 14 C

Lives up to its name only in price. It exceeds 'good' and 'ordinary' by some little margin of taste.

Hautes Cotes de Beaune, Tete de Cuvee, Caves des Hautes Cotes 1995 11 D

James Herrick Cuvee Simone VdP d'Oc 1995 17.5 C

Superb classy stuff. Has texture, weight, balance, length and an overall feel of great natural rich hedgerow fruitiness.

L de La Louviere, Pessac-Leognan 1994 13.5 E

Touch pricey so near ten quid, when it doesn't do justice to its finish for such ostentatious coinage.

L'Enclos Domeque Mourvedre/Syrah VdP d'Oc 1995 15 C

Like a combination of cassis and gravy – terrific texture and richness of flavour. Brilliant arouser of the blood! Suitable for vegans.

Red Burgundy JC Boisset 1995 11 C

Reserve du Musee Bordeaux 1990 14 C

Mature, ripe, positive, individual, untypical, food-friendly.

Saint Joseph, Caves de Saint-Desirat, 1991 14 E

The '93 should be coming into stores as this book comes out (not tasted at time of going to press) but there might be the odd '91 left.

Special Reserve Claret, Cotes de Castillon 1994, Waitrose 14.5 C

Terrific Castillon style exhibiting depth, flavour, richness and controlled, herby rusticity. Deep and dry, yes, but alive with fruit.

St Emilion Yvon Mau 13.5 D

Good but a little unremarkable at six quid.

Winter Hill VdP de l'Aude 1996 14 B

Light, dry, very demure, very drinkable.

FRENCH WINE WHITE

Chablis Gaec des Reugnis 1995 12 E

Chablis Premier Cru Beauregard, Domaine St-Julien 1994 12 E

Chardonnay (Matured in French Oak) VdP d'Oc 1995 14 C

Chardonnay Vin de Pays du Jardin de la France 1995 13 B

Chateau la Chartreuse, Sauternes 1994 (half bottle) 16 E

The texture is so rich and waxy you feel you could chew it for ever. A wonderful pudding wine.

Chateau Terres Douces, Bordeaux 1995 13 D

Too expensive. Okay but hardly thrilling.

Chateau Tour Balot, Premieres Cotes de Bordeaux 1993 13 D

Chateau Vignal Labrie, Monbazillac 1995 15 E

Delicate yet insistent, delicious and brilliant with blue cheese.

Colombard Sauvignon, Comte Tolosan 1996 15.5 C

This is really showing you how advanced these once despised areas of rural viticulture have become. This is a delicious, rich-edged, fruity wine of charm, style and surprising complexity.

Cuckoo Hill Viognier VdP d'Oc 1996 13.5 C

Excellent nutty/lemonic edge on the finish is good, as is the approach. I just wish it was a quid cheaper.

Domaine de la Foret Tete de Cuvee Sauternes 1990 13 G

Silly price.

Domaine de Planterieu VdP des Cotes de Gascogne 1996

It's the gentle sweet-peach lilt on the pineapple fruit which gives it a distant exoticism. Very pleasant tippling here.

Gewurztraminer Cave de Beblenheim 1995, Waitrose

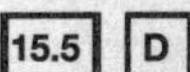

Bursts in the mouth like an exotic gravy of crushed rose-petals. Wonderful way to set up lunch or dinner. Or drink it with Thai/Chinese fish dishes.

James Herrick Chardonnay VdP d'Oc 1995

Le Pujalet Vin de Pays du Gers 1996

Gorgeous peachy/lemon fruit in crisp combination with the acidity. Delicious drinking.

Macon Lugny, Les Charmes 1995

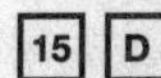

Excellent Macon, as usual from this solid winery. Has flavour, style, balance and those hints of undergrowth which make it typical (but good).

Macon-Villages Chardonnay 1995

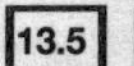

Pinot Blanc d'Alsace Blanck Freres 1996 14.5 C

Rich hints of peach/melon with a crisp undertone of citric acidity make this a superb summer aperitif and fish wine.

Pinot Gris d'Alsace, Cave de Beblenheim 1995 14 D

The smoky apricot fruit is lovely but not as well defined as it might be. Too young still, perhaps. I'd let the wine age for a couple of years yet.

Puligny Montrachet Bernard Grapin 1993 10 G

Sauvignon Calvet, Bordeaux 1996 13.5 C

Fails to clinch a higher rating at the finish.

Sauvignon de Touraine 1996 14 C

Very modern, loose-limbed, relaxed, casually dressed sort of wine – lots of superficial style – for simply opening and throwing back.

Top 40 Chardonnay, VdP d'Oc 1996 16.5 D

Brilliantly priced and very impressive. It represents sophisticated drinking with its depth of fruit – almost opulently rich – and the final flourish of lemon is confident and classy.

White Burgundy Barrel Aged Chardonnay, Boisset 1995 14 C

Creamy, controlled vegetal hints (showing its provenance) and a good wash of flavours over the teeth. If under-a-fiver white burgs like this can flood the land, NZ will have to sit up and take notice.

Winter Hill Dry White VdP de l'Aude 1996 15.5 B

Difficult, with this wine's assertive mineral-sharpened fruit, to imagine anything tastier with fish grimily blackened from the barbie.

Winter Hill Semillon/Chardonnay, VdP de l'Aude 1996 14 C

Has a serious chardonnay edge united with a fun-loving squashed fruit semillon edge. It's a good food wine.

Winter Hill VdP de l'Aude Rose 1996 13.5 B

Delightful little rose, not very meaty but good with fish.

GERMAN WINE WHITE

Avelsbacher Hammerstein Riesling Auslese, Staatsweingut 1989 14 D

O ye of little faith! Worship here!

Geisenheimer Mauerchen Riesling Spatlese, Schloss Schonborn 1989 14.5 D

Controlled kerosene undertones, lovely ripe, plump texture and a honey edge on the finish. A superb summer aperitif.

Kirchheimer Schwarzerde Beerenauslese, Pfalz 1994 (half bottle) 15 C

Longuicher Probstberg Riesling Spatlese, Moselland 1988 14 C

Lemony richness.

Morio Muskat, Pfalz 1995 12.5 B

Serriger Vogelsang Riesling Kabinett, Staatsweingut 1990  C

Good start, fails on the finish to charm so fully.

Urziger Wurzgarten Riesling Spatlese, Monchhof 1993 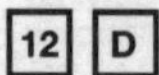

Zeltinger Himmelreich Mosel, Monchhof 1988 

Wonderful value. Drink it for its maturity and unique lemon-sherbet fruit and river-pebble acidity. It's a wonderful summer drink.

GREEK WINE — RED

Vin de Crete Red, Kourtaki 1995 13 B

GREEK WINE — WHITE

Kouros Patras 1994 13 

HUNGARIAN WINE — RED

Deer Leap Sauvignon/Cabernet Franc 1995 14 B

HUNGARIAN WINE — WHITE

Chapel Hill Irsai Oliver, Balaton Boglar 1996

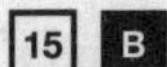

Best vintage yet for this delicate, floral aperitif. It is a brilliant warm-weather, back-garden (or front for that matter) bottle.

Deer Leap Pinot Gris 1995

Tokaji Aszu 5 Puttonyos 1988 (50cl)

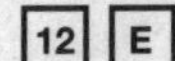

Very, very sweet and highly strung.

ITALIAN WINE — RED

Barolo Nicolello 1992

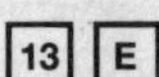

Decent enough until you read the price tag.

Carafe Red Wine, Waitrose (1 litre)

Chianti 1995, Waitrose

Chianti Classico Riserva, Poggio a' Fratti 1991

Lovely baked-earthenware perfume. Dry, rich, earthy fruit of texture and style and a very deep finish of spiced plum which the tannins keep on the teeth and on the tongue. Real class here.

Fiulot Barbera d'Alba, Prunotto 1995 13.5 D

Interesting, very much so, with its fruit, but the finish seems a touch weedy at this price level.

Monica di Sardegna 1995, Waitrose 14 C

A perfect barbecue wine. And light enough to drink with fish.

Montepulciano d'Abruzzo, Umani Ronchi 1995 13 C

It's excellent once it's on the tongue but it hasn't a lot going for it before it gets there or after it disappears down the gullet.

Salice Salentino Riserva, Taurino 1993 13.5 D

I'm not sure the fruit is developing especially winningly. Touch cough-mixture-like at present.

Teroldego Rotaliano, Ca'Vit 1996 15.5 C

Touch of burnt rubber on the perfume only adds to its appeal – which is huge to this tippler. The texture is soft, rubbery, supple, pliant in the mouth and elastic on the finish. It literally rebounds with flavour.

Vino Nobile di Montepulciano, Avignonesi 1993 13 E

A lot of money. Not classy enough for nigh on nine quid.

ITALIAN WINE WHITE

Carafe White Wine, Waitrose (1 litre) 10 C

Frascati Superiore, Villa Rufinella 1995 11 C

Lugana DOC Villa Flora, Zenato 1995 15.5 C

Marche Trebbiano, Moncaro 1996 14 B

Very inexpensive, perfectly cleanly fruity and pleasant, well-balanced, good with food and/or mood. Has a lot going for it.

Nuragus di Cagliari DOC, Sardegna 1995, Waitrose 14.5 C

Orvieto Classico, Cardeto 1995 14 C

Has some immediacy and style. Very fresh and clean with a mineral undertone. Very gluggable.

Pinot Grigio VdT delle Tre Venezie, Fiordaliso 1995 12.5 C

Soave Classico Vigneto Colombara, Zeneto 1995 15 C

Verdicchio dei Casteli Jesi, 1995 13 C

Not bad, certainly respectably clad.

MOROCCAN WINE RED

Chateau Musar 1989 12 E

Looks and smells like a light game and mushroom sauce. The fruit is creaky and sweet – a touch toothless.

NEW ZEALAND WINE RED

Esk Valley Merlot Cabernet Sauvignon, Hawkes Bay 1995

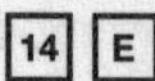

Stylish aromatically and convincing fruit-wise. But nine quid? Hmmm . . .

NEW ZEALAND WINE WHITE

Cooks Chardonnay, Gisborne 1996

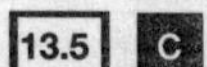

Fails to convince, after a reasonable start, on the finish.

Lawson's Dry Hills Sauvignon Blanc, Marlborough 1996

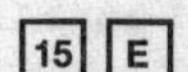

Has a rich thread running through it which never overpowers the delicate acidity. Very stylish.

New Zealand Dry White Wine, Gisborne 1996

Dry and stylish. Attractive price, too.

Villa Maria Private Bin Chardonnay, Gisborne 1995

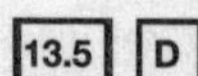

Villa Maria Private Bin Sauvignon, Marlborough 1996

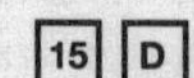

PORTUGUESE WINE RED

Falcoaria Almeirim 1994

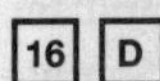

Lovely meaty bouquet – it could come from something knocked up to smother the Sunday roast. The fruit is warm and rich, too.

Ramada Tinto, Estremadura 1995

Light yet rich. Perfect weight of alcohol (11.5%) carrying ripe cherry and plum fruit plus friendly acidity convincingly across the tastebuds.

SOUTH AFRICAN WINE RED

Avontuur Pinotage, Stellenbosch 1996

Benguela Current Merlot, Western Cape 1996

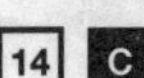

Loads of soupy richness here, softly textured and ripely gluggable. Great fun. Mocks bordeaux with every drop.

Cape Dry Red 1996

Chilled, room temperature, fish, cheese or meat – now, for £3.25, you can't buy better versatility than that. Can you?

Clos Malverne Pinotage Stellenbosch 1996

One of the most insistently savoury pinotages around. It has everything it needs for barbecued food: richness, depth, texture and weight of personality.

Diamond Hills Pinotage/Cabernet Sauvignon 1995 16 C

Brilliant richness and softness held sympathetically by textured tannins. Lovely stuff.

Diemersdal Pinotage 1996 13 D

So showy and evanescent – it's like trying to catch fog.

Fairview Cabernet Franc/Merlot, Paarl 1995 15 D

Smoky aroma leads to quiet fruit which pauses before it slaps and tickles the tastebuds. An excellent summer glug – classy, bright, very beautifully textured.

Klein Constantia Cabernet Sauvignon, Constantia 1993 14 D

Kumala Ruby Cabernet/Merlot 1996 15.5 C

Long Mountain Shiraz 1995 14 C

Cape reds at this price aren't usually this sublimely fruity and full of themselves – in the nicest possible way, of course.

Merwida Winery Ruby Cabernet 1996 15 C

It floods the mouth with richness and savoury depth. A brilliantly flavoured wine of lingering wit and style and high, all-round food compatibility.

Simonsvlei Shiraz Reserve, Paarl 1995 14 C

Extraordinary gun-powdery texture and fruit finish. Terrific to put under a casserole.

Warwick Estate Cabernet Franc 1993 14.5 E

Made by a woman who makes her own decisions – as rare in the South African wine industry as an igloo on the veldt. This wine of hers is rich, ripe and characterful. But it costs.

SOUTH AFRICAN WINE WHITE

Avontuur Le Chardon Chardonnay, Stellenbosch 1996

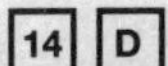

Love the hint of ripe melon and nuts which finishes the wine and what leads up to this is flavourful and attractive. Demure rather than full-blooded.

Cape Dry White, Paarl 1996

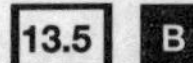

Culemborg Blanc de Noirs 1996

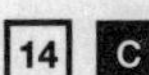

Culemborg Chenin Blanc, Paarl 1996

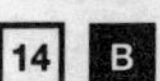

Excellent structure to go with salmon – smoked to poached.

Fairview Chenin Blanc, Paarl 1996

Classy, dry, vigorous, fruity and charming.

KWV Chardonnay 1996

C

Good firm fruit, of richness and depth, and a balanced finish with the edge given to the citric acidity. Stylish stuff.

Landema Falls Chenin Blanc 1996 13 B

Soft and well-priced.

Springfield Estate Chardonnay, Robertson 1996  C

Serious introduction to the fruit (creamy and hints of wood) and a lingering finish. A serious, well-priced chardonnay of character.

SPANISH WINE

RED

Agramont Tinto Tempranillo/Cabernet Sauvignon Crianza, Navarra 1993  

Fabulous union of soft, rich tannins and deep fruit of class and savour. A terrific wine for the money.

Cosme Palacio y Hermanos Rioja 1995 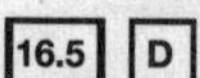 

Simply one of the smoothest riojas around – and it lingers deliciously on the teeth. It has got masses of textured flavour.

Enate Tinto, Somontano 1995 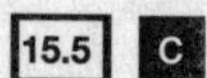 

Excellent price for this rich, deep wine with its gluggability, style and lushly textured ripeness. A superbly well-ordered summer wine for all sorts of foods.

Rioja Crianza, Berberana 1994  

Delicious price, delicious fruit. Not a whit of a sign of old-fashioned rioja coarseness – just smooth rich fruit all the way down.

Stowells of Chelsea Tempranillo (3-litre box)

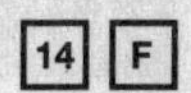

SPANISH WINE — WHITE

Agramont Viura/Chardonnay, Navarra 1995

The texture is creamy, the fruit is firm and full, the finish is stylish, the price is perfect.

Santa Lucia Lightly Oaked Viura 1995

B

USA WINE — RED

Fetzer Valley Oaks Cabernet 1994

Fails to clinch a higher rating – the flavour is there but it nicks the bar as it goes over.

USA WINE — WHITE

Fetzer Sundial Chardonnay, California 1995

Richly textured, buttery, lazy.

FORTIFIED WINE

Apostoles Palo Cortado Muy Viejo, Gonzales Byass (half bottle) 17 E

A fantastically complex sherry which is a wonderful bookworm's treat, or take it to a dinner party as real evidence of your character. It combines leather, melons, almonds and a rich tea-leaf edge of unique unctuosity. It is an extraordinary wine. It is not sweet, rather off-dry. Chill it as a robust end to lunch in the garden.

Churchill's Dry White Port 14 E

Gonzales Byass Apostles (half bottle) 17 E

Magnificent eccentricity of richness yet far from sweetness. Enoch Powell vinified would have this flavour.

Pando Fino, Williams and Humbert 14.5 D

Excellent fino of salinity, nuttiness and pre-war austere cleanliness.

Red Muscadel 1975 14.5 D

Solera Jerezana Dry Oloroso, Waitrose 16.5 D

Fantastic! Rich old classic dry sherry! Uniquely dry, rich, deep, textured and very puzzling – when do you drink it? Bedtime with a book.

White Jerepigo 1979 15 D

SPARKLING WINE/CHAMPAGNE

Cava Brut, Waitrose 16 D

Superb! Clean, nutty, fresh, elegant, brilliantly priced.

Champagne Bredon Brut 14 F

Champagne Brut Blanc de Blancs, Waitrose 15 G

One of the most delicately delicious champagnes around.

Champagne Brut Blanc de Noirs, Waitrose 14.5 F

Champagne Brut Rose, Waitrose 13 G

Champagne Brut Vintage 1989, Waitrose 15.5 G

Champagne Brut, Waitrose 13 E

Chapel Down Century NV (England) 12 D

Clairette de Die Tradition (France) 13.5 D

Cremant de Bourgogne Blanc de Noirs, Lugny 14 D

Cremant de Bourgogne Brut Rose 13 D

Cuvee Royale Brut Blanquette de Limoux 13 D

Duc de Marre Grand Cru Brut 17 G

A real treat which is not absurdly priced. Has old wine in the blend (at least a dozen years old) and this gives biscuity aroma and chewiness to the fruit, almost as pervasive as a fresh baked croissant. Yet it finishes with vigour and purpose.

Green Point Vineyards Brut, Australian 1993 13.5 F

Krone Borealis Brut 1992 (South African) 13.5 D

Le Baron de Beaumont Chardonnay Brut (France) 15 C

Quartet NV, Roederer Estate (California) 14 G

A richer style of bubbly which is much tastier than Bollinger.

Saumur Brut, Waitrose 14 D

Seaview Brut 14 D

Seppelt Great Western Brut 15 C

Silver Swan Sparkling Chardonnay Extra Dry (Hungary) 13.5 C

Flavour and style (to some extent). Decent if not overwhelming.

Waitrose Limited
Customer Service Department
Southern Industrial Area
Bracknell
Berks RG12 8YA
Tel 01344 424680
Fax 01344 862584